MIDNIGHT SUN

Vella Munn

A KISMET® Romance

METEOR PUBLISHING CORPORATION
Bensalem, Pennsylvania

This is for you, Mother, because we share the same love for and awe of Alaska.

VELLA MUNN

Almost nothing in life gives Vella greater pleasure than writing. The joy and hard work of creating something inside her head and heart, bringing characters to life, exploring new worlds and emotions—no wonder she's been doing it for umpteen years and over twenty books. Vella values reader reaction and would appreciate hearing from you. Her address is P. O. Box 98, Jacksonville, OR 97530.

PROLOGUE

First came the rumble, so deep that for perhaps two seconds Brand Lockwood didn't recognize the sound for what it was. Then the noise exploded, shattering the Anchorage, Alaska, spring afternoon.

"Collapse! Run!" he screamed, fighting to be heard above the roar. Acting on instinct, he dove, pushing his solid body off the steel girder he'd been straddling and onto the mound of churned and piled dirt below. He landed on his shoulder and rolled, scrambling for safety. Above him, tons of concrete and steel folded slowly, almost gracefully, in upon itself. Brand was still on his hands and knees when something cold and heavy slammed into him and sent him sprawling. With dust and dirt in his lungs, and the air filled with a thunderous roar, he clawed at the earth, desperately dragging himself out from under whatever had attacked him.

Freedom! Nothing mattered except that.

Despite his ripped nails, Brand kept at his task. His breath came in short, hard gasps; he fought panic. Not again! No. It couldn't be happening again! As the roar died and thick dust filled the air, he rose on unsteady legs, ignoring the hot pain in his right thigh. He turned. What had once been a skeleton of a parking garage now had become a graveyard of rubble.

Silence hung around him. It seemed to have a life of its own. He could see people running and sensed their urgency, but all sound had been switched off. For as long as it took for him to draw dusty air into his lungs, he heard nothing, saw nothing, except the gray Alaskan sky and destruction. He almost laughed, almost. This high-rise going up in Anchorage wasn't his project. But, driven by a lesson that still, occasionally, gave him nightmares, he'd felt compelled to interfere. He'd tried to convince the builder that concrete reinforced with the newest advances in rebar and polymer wasn't a luxury but a necessity for the rest of the project. His entreaty had fallen on deaf ears. And now—

Now.

Someone screamed. The cry echoed and was followed by another.

He couldn't stand here, not with workers trapped in the rubble. He took a step. His right leg almost collapsed under him. He grabbed at his thigh, feeling torn flesh instead of denim. Whatever the damage, it could wait. For now, nothing existed except the massive, ruined Tinkertoy he'd been climbing a few minutes ago. He wouldn't let what happened years ago root him where he was.

"Get some ambulances!" someone screamed. "Equipment! We're going to need equipment."

Equipment? Brand's head swam. It would take cranes and bulldozers to move the massive broken concrete slabs and twisted steel, but bringing the equipment into place, determining where and how to dig would take time. And there might be trapped men and women who didn't have that luxury.

Think! He couldn't remember seeing more than a handful of workers on the structure with him. But those who had been—

"Are you all right?"

Brand turned to see a young man in a business suit scrambling over debris toward him. He opened his mouth to answer when a sharp cry rang out. Side by side, Brand and the businessman sprinted forward and dropped to their knees beside what they could see of a worker with a reddish, dirt-caked beard. Brand's thigh felt on fire; he fought to ignore it.

"My legs!" the worker cried. "Get me out!"

The businessman shot Brand a desperate look. "I can't see his legs," he babbled. "They're under—"

Brand looked around, his mind clicking into gear. A lifetime ago when the other nightmare happened, he'd been a scared kid, barely a breath away from throwing up or passing out or both. Now he knew what had to be done. The worker's lower body was pinned by a thick, flat slab of concrete. If they had something to pry with, they might be able to free him. Scrambling to his feet, Brand clamped his hand over his thigh, hurried over to a length of steel, and wrestled it into place. With the businessman and two newcomers to lend their weight, the slab shuddered and lifted enough for a husky woman in a jogging outfit to drag the worker out from under it. A moment later two men who identified themselves as off-duty firemen took over. One of them pointed at Brand's leg.

"You're bleeding. Hold on. The ambulances will be here in a few minutes."

Brand didn't want anything to do with ambulances or hospitals—ever again. Grunting, he turned away and forced his grit-filled eyes to focus. The collapsed structure looked like an ant hill with would-be rescuers scrambling over it. He could walk away now, get off by himself, give shock the time it demanded.

"I hear something."

Brand looked down at the husky woman in the jogging outfit. "What?" he asked.

"Listen. I hear—" She pointed at a loose pile of cement. "Someone's in there."

Brand shook his head to clear it of the sound of his pounding heart. As the woman continued to point, he stepped closer, his thigh knotting.

"Please. Please."

For the second time since clawing his way out from under what could have been his grave, Brand dropped to his knees. He saw a hand, only a hand. The woman drew back. "No," she whispered. "Oh no. He's dead."

Another strangled plea coming from under the pile convinced Brand that the opposite was true. His mind shifted in a direction he didn't want it to go, and he all too easily imagined what the owner of that hand was going through—trapped, scared, surrounded by darkness so deep it seemed to have no end. "Get someone over here, *now*!" he ordered. "Shovels. We're going to need shovels." Because he didn't trust his leg to support him again, he settled his weight on his left hip and clamped his dirty fingers around the hand. The buried man gripped back.

"I'm here," he said as the woman whirled and ran. "I'm not leaving you. Do you hear me? We're getting help."

"Please."

"Talk to me," he pressed, his heart thudding. "Can you breathe? How do you feel?"

"My chest. It's—something's broken."

Brand continued to squeeze the man's hand, the seconds slogging by like the hand on an unwound clock. Because he didn't want to deplete the man's strength any more than necessary, he didn't ask questions. Instead he kept up a running commentary about the rescue work going on around him, telling the trapped man that it was starting to look like an ambulance convention. The words weren't important. Maybe, as long as he held the man's hand, he could keep him from giving in to panic. When the woman jogger returned with a half dozen rescuers on her heels, he told the man that, too. Then the sound of shovels filled the air, and he could only hold on.

Ten, fifteen minutes later—he couldn't measure time— the workers dug down enough that he saw a battered silver hardhat, dust-caked boots, filthy jeans. Because the rescuers were afraid of inflicting more damage with their tools, the man's torso remained covered. Brand leaned forward and with his free hand wiped the man's face. He looked to be barely twenty, brown eyed, bearded. His mouth was open; Brand heard him breathing. So young, the way he'd been.

"Just a little longer," Brand reassured him around a growing knot of rage. This didn't have to happen. Damn it, it didn't! "They've got to take it easy so they don't hurt you. Hell of a way for the day to turn out, isn't it?"

"Yeah." The young man coughed; his face contorted with pain. "I'm scared."

"You want to know something? I'm not doing so hot myself."

"Yeah?" The man blinked. "No kidding?"

"We'd have to be pretty stupid not to have been frightened. Look, they're digging with their hands now. It'll be slow going, but they're getting there. About your chest. You still think something's broken?"

"I—don't know. Don't leave me. Please."

Although he'd told himself that right now it was essential for him to be strong for this kid, his nervous system hadn't received the message. How long had they been holding hands while he tried to give the trapped man the strength he needed? Long enough to remember that horrible long ago day when he'd been the one trapped. "I'm not leaving," he promised as his rage and frustration swirled around him. "As long as you need me, I'm here.

You can talk? It isn't going to hurt too much?'' When the man shook his head, he forced a smile. "What's your name?"

"Hank. Hank Crayton."

An icy chill slashed through him, clashing with his anger. "Crayton? Your father—"

"Art. He's—this is his—he's the builder."

"I know." He forced out the words. *Damn! Damn. If only Art Crayton had listened!*

"Where—" Hank swallowed and his face contorted. "Dad's here today. He—is he all right?"

At this moment, Brand didn't give a damn whether Art Crayton was alive or not. "You worry about you," he told the kid. "In a few minutes they'll load you in an ambulance and haul you off to the hospital. You'd better make sure those nurses clean you up." He wiped at Hank's face again, thinking that Crayton's incompetence or greed, or whatever word fit, had nearly killed his son.

In that moment, he made himself a vow. Never again would Crayton jeopardize a life. He forced a smile. "The way you look, you're going to scare your girlfriend half to death. You got a girlfriend? Tell me about her."

"No girlfriend. Just—she's going to—"

"Who's going to what?" he pressed, afraid Hank's silence meant he was passing out.

"My sister," Hank cracked. "Please tell her I'm all right. Dad's going to need her."

To hell with what Art Crayton needed. And Hank's sister—he hoped to hell she made her father face what he'd done. "Here we go. Yeah. That's the last of it. Time for you to head for the hospital." Brand squeezed again and blinked, feeling grit. "Hank? What kind of flowers do you like?"

"Flowers?" The kid's voice trailed off. "You'd send me flowers?"

"Why not? Maybe candy. Anything you like."

"I don't—thank you."

Brand rocked back on his heels, pain arching from his thigh clear to the top of his head. *Thank you*. The words echoed inside him. He'd never hear that again from a Crayton.

Not that he wanted to. It was too damn late for Art Crayton to say anything. "I'm sorry" wasn't enough. It never would be.

ONE

The mountains intimidated Kara Richardson. Fear had seldom made an impact in her life, but these great shaded monsters with deep pockets of ice packed into their valleys couldn't be ignored. Skagway, last stop on the Inside Passage, looked so flat and small, so vulnerable by comparison. Even with its freshly painted buildings, the evergreens flanking the small commercial core, and early morning visitors peering into store windows, she couldn't shake the sense that the Klondike-era gold town had been separated from the rest of the world.

Kara tried not to think about the isolation. It was mid-May. When and if her brother and father needed her, she could leave here a number of ways. The pilot who'd brought her here recommended one of the cruise ships that churned up and down the icy-gray Lynn Canal—if there was any extra space and if she had the time. The road leading to Whitehorse would work, if she had a vehicle. Otherwise, chartering a plane, although expensive, was the final alternative.

Alternatives. The word rang through her head like a sick joke. Options were something she didn't have, not if she was going to support her family and, please, learn the truth behind that horrible day three weeks ago.

As she walked along the weathered boardwalk flanking historic buildings that housed gift shops and restaurants, she fought the knot in her stomach. Maybe she was the biggest fool in the biggest state in the nation to be heading toward the construction trailer at the north end of town. For all she knew, the moment Brand Lockwood heard who she was, she'd be without a job and without the money to get home—without understanding Lockwood's role in the nightmare her family had been trapped in.

But she'd go through with it because doing nothing was incomprehensible.

And, somehow, she'd weather what Lockwood told her about her father.

Turning right, she left the small commercial area and headed toward the outskirts of town. Because she had to walk, she'd left the lodge a good half hour before her appointment. Walking also gave her the time she needed with her nerves. As she neared her destination, a large, cluttered lot next to a warehouse of some kind, she took a deep breath. It would take a lot more than an early morning stroll to put her life back on course.

The trailer she had been told to report to wasn't more than five or six years old, but time hadn't been kind to it. Its original color had been sanded away by the elements and little attempt had been made to keep it level. But why bother? She, the rest of the crew, and their boss, would be working on a mountain, not down here. The wooden stairs leading to the side door settled uneasily under her weight. The small sign bearing the no-nonsense word "Construction" had been screwed into place, but one of the screws had worked loose, canting the metal rectangle. She had no idea what waited inside, but whatever came of the meeting, she'd survive it.

She lifted her hand to knock, then paused, her attention

momentarily drawn to the small silver band on her little finger. At eight, the ring, a gift from her mother, had been a perfect fit. It, like the cameo necklace resting against her throat, served as precious memories of Holly Crayton. Wondering if her mother might somehow be watching, protecting, Kara knocked on the door.

"Come on in."

Kara sucked in a breath of chilled, salt-tasting air and turned the handle. For a moment the door stuck, then when she pushed on it, it jerked open. The interior, lit by a bright overhead light, was filled with the trappings of the construction business: tool boxes, hard hats, a hand cart, two-way radios, blueprints, product samples, and directly under the light, a wooden desk large enough to accommodate the stack of papers on it. Behind the desk stood a man, a large, silent, black-haired man who studied every nuance of her approach with dark, unwavering eyes.

He belonged here, she decided in a heartbeat. He was as much a part of this world of strength and endurance as any eagle soaring over snow-cloaked mountains. He might not know the first thing about big city survival, but his body had been honed by the elements and physical labor. Whatever his job required, he was equal to it.

"Brand Lockwood?" she asked. She kept her hands by her side, her fingers dangling loose in an attempt to present a picture of confidence. This was the man who'd saved her brother's life and then turned around and destroyed her father's. What was she supposed to feel?

Off balance.

Alive.

"That's right. You're . . ." He glanced down, then looked at her again. Maybe looked beneath the surface. "Kara Richardson?"

"Yes."

"I thought so. I've got two other women coming in

today, but they're not due until afternoon. That pretty well narrows it down."

She nodded, then came closer, side-stepping a generator. Richardson. Was the name all that remained of a little more than a year of marriage, high hopes and sober reality? Forcing her mind off the thought, she concentrated on the man she hoped would give her employment—and more.

Brand Lockwood wore a flannel shirt rolled up at the sleeves to show hardened forearms covered with a dark dusting of hair. The shirttail had been tucked into jeans that had seen countless washings and been molded to his frame. He was broad at the shoulders, broader than most men. He narrowed down to a slim waist and flat belly before his solid thighs repeated the message of strength in his chest and arms. She judged him to be a shade over six feet. Hank had told her Lockwood was in his mid-thirties. Without knowing that, she would have had to estimate his age at anywhere from twenty-five to forty. His physique said twenty-five. His eyes, dark and digging, had seen much more of life than that.

No. She couldn't tell him who she was. Not yet.

Lockwood swept a broad hand over the cramped trailer, his eyes not losing contact with hers. She knew he'd taken his measure of her. What he thought of her blue turtleneck and worn jeans, or what conclusions he'd come to about her lean, athletic body she couldn't guess. But she sensed that he'd soon tell her whether he thought her equal to the job. "Sit down, if you can find room," he said in a voice that came from the depths of his chest. "I'll be taking most of this equipment up the mountain tomorrow, but until then we're going to have to put up with being crammed in here."

Glancing around, she spotted a wooden chair on which a case of motor oil rested. She gripped the box and dropped it to the floor with a thunk. She sat, her features carefully composed. The trailer, the equipment, most of all the man commanding her attention said *male*. Because this was the only world she'd ever known, she had no desire to try to soften her own image. "I've always thought that's the hardest part, the waiting, the gearing up," she said, falling back on a thousand conversations stretching through the fabric of her life. "When I talked to you, you said you were getting a late start."

"A few days later than I'd intended. Something had priority. You've had time to think about what we're doing here? No second thoughts?"

Oh yes. Second and third and fourth thoughts. "I'm fascinated by what you're taking on," she told him. "Building a road over permafrost. I've never done that."

Lockwood grunted; there was no other way to describe the sound coming from him. "It's a new one for me, too. The technology is just getting off the ground. That's why all this." He indicated a couple of thick, worn folders. "Between you and me, I'm running this by the seat of my pants."

"Are you?" she asked because something was expected of her.

"Pretty much. Most of my previous work has been with buildings. Now I'm branching out to other things. Challenging myself." He again nodded at the papers on the desk and sat down, his body taut as if wanting action. "I'm going to need glasses if I do much more research. It's time to put this textbook knowledge to practical use. Basically, what we'll do is put slabs of styrofoam between the earth and paving materials."

"Sytrofoam? Interesting."

"I thought so. Through trial and error they've learned that the best thing to do with permafrost is leave it alone. Only, it's a little more complicated than that. What I have to do is properly identify the varieties of permafrost and know how to deal with them." He smiled ruefully. "As

I'm sure you know, the construction world is constantly changing. Improvements in materials and design are always being developed. A builder who doesn't keep up is shortchanging his client." He leaned forward, eyes intent on her. "And sometimes jeopardizing the lives of his employees."

Despite the ice that suddenly coursed through her veins at his hard-spoken words, Kara nodded. "I know," she said, unable to think of anything else.

"Do you?" His eyes held her, grew darker. "Have you ever heard a building going down? Heard the scream of someone trapped? I've gone through it twice. After the first time, I swore it would never happen again. But—" He ran a big, weathered hand over his eyes. "You don't want to hear this. I should talk business, not force you to listen to me rant and rave. I'm trying to remember. Weren't you in Anchorage when you called? What brings you here?"

Kara made herself smile. For some incomprehensible reason, his gesture made her wonder what a smile would look like on him. Rich and warm? "The money. No one can top what you're offering."

"I won't argue that. That's the only way I can get enough qualified people to come up to the end of nowhere. Anchorage? You couldn't find work there?"

Because she'd guessed the question would be asked, she had already come up with an explanation, one that, while not an out-and-out lie, sidestepped the real issue. "What I'd signed on for, at the last minute things didn't work out. I called around, heard about your project. Like you said, it sounded like a fascinating challenge. Besides, I'm a bit of a history buff. I've always wondered what the Klondike was like during the gold rush. Hopefully I'll have time to do some research and exploring." *Did that matter?*

"Hm." Lockwood leaned back. The gesture expanded

his chest and put stress on his shirt buttons. "What it took to survive back then, why so many risked everything to come here, whether it was worth it, I can't say. I don't know how much time you're going to have to try to come up with the answers." He leaned forward, making her grateful for the barrier between them, in some insane way making her wish it didn't exist. "This is hard work, as I'm sure you know. Six, sometimes seven days a week. With the kind of daylight they get up here during the summer, we'll be putting in some killer hours."

Kara nodded to let her new boss know she understood. The time frame for getting the job done had come up during the telephone conversation that ended with her being hired. She only hoped he wouldn't ask about the job that had "fallen through." If pushed for an answer, would she lie, evade? *No.* Even if he had struck her as a man who would tolerate evasion, it wasn't in her.

As Brand stood and riffled through a shelf to his left, looking for an example of the kind of styrofoam they'd be using, Kara took advantage of the silence to concentrate on the man—as if she hadn't been doing just that already.

He wasn't handsome. A man that strong, that toughened by the elements could never be called that. There was a fierceness to him, almost as if he'd been backed into a corner and come out swinging. He might not know what or why he fought. He might not care. But as long as he breathed, that intensity would remain part of him.

Without that, a great chunk would be missing from what he was.

Fighting the impulse to run her palms over her jeans, she acknowledged the man's impact on her senses. She hadn't expected this, hadn't prepared herself for it. But no matter how much she might try to deny it, Brand Lockwood exuded a message of sensuality that couldn't be ignored. An aura of masculinity was part and parcel of every inch of him: his strong chin and deeply tanned throat, the way his hip bones thrust against jeans cast in his body's mold, the wide splay of his muscled legs. Maybe most of all, that message lay in deepset eyes so profoundly blue that they were almost black. Eyes like that were capable of reaching deep inside a woman. And maybe finding the truth.

Touching a woman's vulnerabilities and needs.

Brand—she no longer thought of him as Lockwood—turned back around, fixing his gaze on her again. She clamped down on an involuntary shudder and waited for him to speak. After another few seconds during which he did nothing more than look at her, he did. "What this project is all about is improving the road leading out of Skagway," he said. "At White Pass we're into Canada, so from there on, the Klondike Highway is their domain. But those few miles heading up into the mountains from here are a real challenge. We'll be working through everything from a rain forest zone to subarctic alpine tundra, so forget everything you think you know about road construction. You said you've worked on roads before, didn't you?"

She nodded. Because she'd already told him she could run every piece of machinery involved in road construction, she saw no reason to go over that again. Instead she sketched some of the projects she'd been part of.

"If I checked your background, it'd all be there?"

She straightened but felt no surge of anger. They were strangers. As a man whose reputation as well as his business was on the line, he'd have to ask hard questions. "I know what I'm doing," she assured him. "I wouldn't be here if I didn't."

"You didn't answer my question, Ms. Richardson. Your background. You haven't left anything out?"

"Like what?"

"Like, you aren't wanted for anything, are you?"

She blinked. "What?"

"It wouldn't be the first time I've had a worker with a reason to isolate himself."

"No," she said slowly, softly. "I'm not running."

"There's running and then there's running, Ms. Richardson. I hire women. That's never been an issue with me. But put yourself in my position. Out of the blue, I get a call from a stranger with exactly the skills I need. Then you show up, young, attractive, a lot younger than I expected."

When she simply looked at him, he went on. "I'm not going to ask personal questions, if that's what you're worried about. Everyone's entitled to privacy, to their own lives. I'm just a little surprised and curious. That's all."

"I didn't know my age would be a consideration," she countered.

"Didn't you? It's never come up before?"

It seldom had. Most of the time she worked with her father. The few times she'd done something on her own, she'd proudly taken her family background along as reference. Now it was different. "I guess I don't give my age that much thought," she explained.

"Don't you? I don't often hear someone say that." He looked thoughtful for a moment. "Look, have you found a place to stay?"

"Not really. I flew in about dark last night. The bush pilot I hired knows the owner of one of the hotels. They found a bed for me, but I'm going to have to nail down something permanent. And I need to buy a truck."

Brand started to lean his elbows on the cluttered table and then drew back as if needing to distance himself from the paperwork. "The truck shouldn't be a problem. I think everyone who lives here has at least four vehicles. As for a place to stay . . ." He broke eye contact with her and rummaged through the papers by his telephone with broad, impatient fingers. "Yeah. Here it is. I've had a few residents come to me, offering to put up my workers. It doesn't sound as if most of those places are much, trailers, cabins, even a tent. But this one might work." He held up a piece of paper that bore the smear of an oily fingerprint. "You're here alone aren't you? No family?"

"No family. I'm divorced. And I don't have children."

Brand nodded, his eyes unwavering, questioning. "I hope this works out for you. I think it might." His features softened. "I was having dinner in one of the cafés the other night and got into a conversation with an older couple. They live across a creek from town. There are two places on their property. The way they described it, the unoccupied one is a cabin. Apparently the bridge over the creek took quite a beating last winter so you can't drive across it, but if you don't mind walking about a quarter of a mile, they'd like the company." He opened his mouth as if to say more, then closed it.

"Company? They really want a renter, don't they?" she asked, relieved that they'd slid so easily over her family ties.

"I think that's a secondary consideration." For the first time since she stepped into the trailer, a smile touched Brand's face. She liked, was intrigued by, the transformation. "They're pretty isolated out there. Apparently the old man's brother used to live in the cabin, but he took a vacation to Florida and never came back. As you're probably guessing, it doesn't take much for these two to tell you their life history. I got the feeling the woman's a little leery of having some scruffy construction worker a few feet away. They'd feel safer with you. And, well—"

Don't do this to me, she thought when he didn't go on. She wanted absolutely nothing except a working relationship with Brand Lockwood. If they started talking about the needs and fears of this old couple, if he said anything more to make her believe he was a caring person, how would she remain detached from him? But even as she asked the question, she knew distance from her boss wasn't what she and her brother, even her father, needed. If she was going to fully understand what caused the parking garage to collapse, she and Brand would have to reach beyond the almost nonexistent relationship they now had.

"Thank you. I'll talk to them," she said. "And, hopefully, find an old truck. As long as I can get my hands on the parts, I can probably make it run."

"I hope so."

Despite the unsettling impact of his unwavering eyes, Kara kept her desire to leave under check. No matter what she felt inside, she wouldn't let him guess at the effort. "You sound as if you don't believe me," she said, her voice firm.

"I'm reserving judgment, Ms. Richardson. I've hired and then had to fire more than one person who overstated his, or her, skills. If I find out you can't cut it, I'll tell you."

She straightened her spine and met his eyes. "I can. After all, I've been in this business my entire life."

"Have you?"

Thrown off balance by the curt words, she decided to wait him out. Brand ran a hand over his right thigh, wincing as he did. Oh no! Had he been hurt in the accident? "I think," he said, "this is something you and I need to get straight, today. I have four other women on the crew. All of them are locals used to hard work. You don't look the part."

This wasn't the first time she had heard that. True, she was slender, but beneath lay muscles accustomed to physical labor. If he looked at her hands he would see short nails, long, strong fingers. She might not be able to singlehandedly shove a boulder out of the road, but she could guide a bulldozer to do the task, and if the bulldozer balked, she could battle the machinery until it did her bidding. "I applied for the job because I know I can handle it. I think . . ." She leaned forward, using the gesture to telegraph the message that he didn't intimidate her. "You should give me a chance before you judge me."

"I'm not judging, Ms. Richardson. I just want both of us to have all our cards on the table."

She pushed herself to her feet. *Tell him. Just get it out.* But she couldn't, not now. First she had to clamp on a hardhat and put in enough hours to draw a paycheck. Her family *had* to have money to live on. Hopefully in a few days she'd have earned her boss's respect. Once she'd done that, she'd tell him who she was.

She couldn't risk anything yet. "Please call me Kara," she said. "Mr. and Ms. don't have much place on a construction site."

Brand too rose, his physique dwarfing the desk. "No. They don't. I'll see you tomorrow, Kara."

Then, before she could turn away, he stepped around his desk and thrust out his hand. After a hesitation that lasted no longer than a heartbeat, she answered the challenge.

She was right. This was the hand of a man who wrestled his way through life. Who backed down from nothing.

Who, although he had no right, somehow reached beyond flesh and muscle and heated her blood.

She'd been gone only a few seconds when Brand gave up the pretense that he gave a damn about trying to bring some semblance of order to his desk. When Kara Richardson called to ask for a job, he'd been a little surprised, not that a woman wanted to do highway construction, but that she'd been able to get in touch with him when he'd just gotten to Skagway. Then she explained that she'd been doing construction in the Northwest most of her life, and he understood.

Word got around in this business. Word of mouth brought him more employees than any ad or referral agency ever had. He'd been prepared for a warhorse of a woman capable of holding her own in this rough and sometimes dangerous work. That was the kind of employee he needed. Male or female, those he hired had to be capable of handling the demanding physical labor.

Kara Richardson was no warhorse.

Brand rested his sensitized right hand on his injured thigh, seeking to still the memory of the femininity that simmered beneath her firm handshake. His wound was still tender but healing rapidly enough that it shouldn't hold him back on the site. And once the tear stopped hurting, maybe he wouldn't relive the accident in dreams that soaked the bed with his sweat and reminded him of the fragility of life. If nothing else, Kara might serve as a distraction from what he wished to hell had never happened.

She hadn't said much about her personal life and obviously didn't want to answer questions. For reasons that were none of his business, Kara Richardson needed time by herself. That, he guessed, was what had brought her here, not the money. Well, she wouldn't be the first woman who wanted to put distance between herself and some man.

Despite a quiet, permanent strength that was part of her, she'd be vulnerable, or scarred, or scared, or all three. She might jump into a relationship with one of the other workers as a way of healing her emotional wounds. He'd seen it before. But he didn't think so. Nothing about the way she carried or conducted herself hinted at a woman on the make.

She couldn't do anything about those big, black, provocative eyes, just as he supposed, short of cutting it off, she couldn't do much about the rich coil of dark hair trailing down her back. She wore little makeup, just enough to accent her lashes and brows. He'd noticed her silver ring and cameo necklace, wondering at those touches of femininity. Wanting to touch the creamy hollow where the necklace rested.

The turtleneck shirt revealed more than a hint about her high, rounded breasts, the ladder of her ribs, her narrow waist. Being built along graceful, limber lines wasn't a crime any more than wearing jewelry was. Her jeans faithfully followed her contours from curving hips to strong thighs and long, slender legs. What could she do about that? Wear baggy coveralls?

The woman had gotten to him. Just like that.

Unsettled, Brand paced to a small open window. He sucked in a deep breath of incredibly clean air, facing facts. This was one employee he wouldn't be able to dismiss at the end of the day.

Nothing might come of it, but he was damn glad he'd been able to tell her about the little cabin. A woman alone, especially a young, attractive woman, needed a safe place to live. Just thinking about her staying within shouting distance of the older couple made him feel better.

A good deed, he told himself. That's all it was, a good deed.

From a man who'd always made it a point not to invade his employees' private lives? Right.

He could see her now, a small, retreating figure dwarfed by her immense surroundings. She walked slowly, head held high, hands . . . wait. The hands that had rested so easily by her side were now knotted into tight fists.

Why? Was it something he'd said, buttons he'd pushed?

What did it matter? As long as she did her job, he'd pay her salary, nothing more.

He'd taken his other employees at their word. Unless he saw something he didn't like, he wouldn't get in touch with the references she'd given him or verify what she'd said about her work history. Her past, like his, had no place in the present. Only doing the job, as a team, did.

He turned from the window and returned to his desk,

seeking distraction. As he leafed through the material on it, his attention was drawn to a report he'd been distributing to others in the business on the benefits of adding polymeric admixtures to wet concrete for strength. If other contractors read the report and incorporated the product, the entire industry would benefit.

Most contractors, thank heavens, were conscientious enough that they embraced whatever made their structures safer. It was only men like Art Crayton who insisted on doing things the familiar way, or worse, cut corners that didn't dare be cut.

Brand leaned back in his chair and closed his eyes. For an instant the image of long black hair and coal-like eyes distracted him. He shook off the sensual image and thought about the collapse again.

There's no proof, he reminded himself, aware that his rage of three weeks ago had turned into something manageable. Until the investigation was complete, he wouldn't lay the blame at Crayton's feet. It was possible that once the inspectors were done with their high-frequency sound waves, X-rays, and microscopic examinations they'd find that the collapse had been beyond Crayton's control.

Maybe.

Kara had to ask questions of a half dozen people before she found someone who could direct her to the dirt road leading to where Cliff and Ada Bostian lived. Brand had been right. The wooden bridge over the narrow, silt-bottomed creek was so weak that she felt uneasy just walking over it. As soon as she crossed the creek, a large black dog appeared, his head low, growling. She stopped, breathing shallowly as the dog approached. When he was a few feet away, she cautiously held out her hand. A moment later a large, wet tongue slid over her fingers.

"You're a phony, you know that, don't you?" Her question so excited the dog that his tail beat against his flanks. "All you want is a little company. Are the folks home? What do you think? Think you and I could get along for the summer?"

The question stopped her. Until now she hadn't tried to project beyond whatever time it took to earn what her family needed to live on . . . and to hear Brand Lockwood's side of things. But Brand had hired her because he needed someone with her skills. Her relationship with the man might be incredibly complex—it certainly already was for her. But for Brand, things were simple. He needed a full crew doing their jobs.

She was part of that crew.

But what else? How would she fill her off work hours?

"Be glad you're a dog," she told the Lab who led the way back down the narrow road that cut through a wind-bent stand of alder surrounded by pines. "It's easier if all you have to worry about is being fed and having a warm place to sleep."

The house the dog trotted up to was pretty much what she expected. Made from rough-cut logs, it sported a tin roof and a chimney from which smoke swirled in the wind. Someone had built a small porch, but it looked only a little sturdier than the bridge. The open shed held less than a cord of wood. Through the dense evergreens, she spotted the outline of another, crudely built building.

"You lost?"

Kara jumped at the sound, then regained her composure as a man with a full head of white hair and equally rich white beard appeared. He leaned heavily on his cane, his eyes bright and friendly. He looked as if a sudden wind would knock him over. Smiling, she explained what she was doing here.

"I remember. Ada—that's my wife—she said that man, Lockwood, was going to give himself an ulcer if he didn't stop to chew his food. She heard him talking to the waitress and figured straight out that he was someone important on that road job. She said he looked lonely sitting there all by himself. I told her he had a lot on his mind and wanted to be alone, but . . ." Cliff Bostian whistled through what were left of his teeth, calling the dog to his side. "Ada's always worrying about people. Worries about me till I can hardly take a breath without her asking if I did it all right. Thinks I should move into town."

"What do you think?" Kara asked around the smile that threatened to break free. Cliff, who she loved immediately, could barely get around. No wonder Brand's voice had been full of concern when he talked about the elderly couple.

"I think I'd rather be six feet under than shoulder to shoulder with everyone and their third cousin. You saw Skagway. The place's a madhouse, particularly this time of the year."

She didn't see a few hundred visitors in that light, but she guessed the elderly man wanted her to agree with him. "I suppose it depends on how you look at it," she started. Before she could say more, the front door opened and a woman stepped out. Cliff Bostian probably wasn't an inch over five feet and couldn't weigh much more than 100 pounds. Ada Bostian weighed at least half again what her husband did and was several inches taller.

"What are you doing, old man?" Ada challenged. "I can't take my eyes off you for a minute. Flirting with some pretty young thing, are you? You ought to be ashamed." Ada shot Kara a broad grin. "You have to watch a man when he gets senile like this one is. There's no knowing what he gets in his head. Probably going to need a pacemaker just from talking to you."

Kara laughed, then explained what she was doing here. The words were barely out of her mouth before she saw relief in Ada's eyes.

"Cliff didn't want me bothering Mr. Lockwood," the buxom woman explained after a mock glare at her husband. "He said no one'd want to come out here, especially with the bridge out. But I figured it was worth a shot what with the size of the crew and all. Would you like to see the place? It isn't much."

Ada was right. The inside of the tin roof cabin had never really been finished. Although it was well-insulated, plasterboard lined the interior walls. It consisted of a single, large room with a sleeping area at one end, something that passed for a kitchen at the other, and a small living room in the middle. Cliff told her that the one door led to a bathroom. "Hot water," he told her proudly. "Frank and I, that's my brother, we put in the shower and toilet by ourselves."

Ada glared at her husband. "Who put in the sink? Men. Always exaggerating. Are you handy, Kara? What I'm saying is, if you want this place, anything you want to do to fix it up is just fine with us."

Kara took a minute to tap the side of the stove pipe. "I want to clean that out. It sounds as if there might be a pretty good layer of creosote in there."

"I kept telling Frank to run a chain down it, but he's the laziest thing. It's a good thing he moved to where they don't need heat. Cliff doesn't like heights and I'm—well, it takes a little more agility and less weight than I have to get up on that roof. What do you think?" she asked, her eyes anxious.

Kara wanted to say yes, but not until she'd asked one more question. "Is there a telephone out here?"

"Not in the cabin. Frank, he didn't make many calls and when he did, he used ours. Cheap, that's what he was. Always forgetting to pay his share of the bill. I can tell just looking at you that that won't be a problem. You can have all the privacy you need."

Privacy meant less to her than knowing there'd be someone around to answer the phone in case her father or brother needed to reach her. She explained that she didn't expect to have much more use for a phone than Frank had, but it was essential that she remain in touch with her family.

Ada cocked her head. "No boyfriend?"

"I'm divorced," she said simply. Then, because she hadn't had a woman to talk to for a long time, the rest came out. "He wasn't crazy about what I did for a living, among other things."

"What was it, honey? He try to remake you?"

Kara looked up, surprised by Ada's intuition. "Not completely. He just wanted—he never could understand why I wouldn't quit construction to manage his office." She stopped, working her way past the residue of emotion she felt for Scott.

"Then it's time you started looking for someone new. Healthy young woman like you shouldn't be alone. First day on the job and you'll probably be beating them off with a stick."

"I doubt that. From what I understand, we're going to be pretty busy."

"There's always time for certain things, if you know what I mean. Problem is, most of the men around here don't know how to treat a lady." Ada gave her husband a teasing grin. "And if you have a dress, stockings, and makeup, you'd really set them on their ears. Maybe remind them that there's such a thing as manners."

"I didn't bring a dress, or stockings."

"Hm. Well—" Ada cocked her head again, giving her a thorough looking over. "You probably wouldn't need to dress up anyway and from what I know of those pantyhose things, they're not worth the effort. One look at you and the men'll start coming around; don't you worry about that. Like that contractor fellow." Ada sighed dramatically and placed her hand over her breast. "He's all man, isn't he? I'd have to be six feet under not to be aware of that."

Kara shrugged. "I didn't notice."

"Didn't you? Maybe you're just telling yourself you didn't see anything. Well, sometimes it's right being on your own. I was thirty before I let this old goat corral me. Things change once a body gets married. We start depending on someone."

"I guess. I wasn't married long," Kara said simply. "I didn't really depend on Scott, certainly not as much as he wanted me to." *I tried to be what he wanted. I just didn't know how.*

"That's the problem with men." Ada snorted. "They think we can read their minds and there's nothing we'd like better than twisting ourselves into pretzels trying to do what they want. Take it from me, there's nothing like a man for making a woman crazy. Only, if I was younger, single, I don't know if I could ignore that Lockwood fellow. Like I said, he's all man."

Yes. He is.

TWO

There didn't appear to be any soil in the mountain the crew would spend the summer on. But it had to be there or the weather-stunted evergreens reaching for the grayed sky wouldn't have found what they needed to sustain life. Civilization had made a fragile mark on the wilderness, a steep, narrow road which went from sea level to 3,000 feet in less than fifteen miles. Kara, waiting to begin work, was in awe of whomever had first attacked this seemingly impenetrable monster.

Then Brand, his weight braced against the engine housing of a rear dump hauler, began speaking. A half-dozen muttered conversations ceased. Kara tucked her hands in her jeans pockets, assessing the man in charge of this experienced, work-ready crew.

"I don't suppose I have to point out the obvious. The way the road is now, it simply isn't doing the job," Brand said. "This is the only land route in or out of Skagway. To meet current and anticipated demands, the entire road needs to be straightened, widened, and blacktopped. As I see it, the greatest challenge will be a half dozen sharp switchbacks."

35

Kara inched forward so she could hear above the wind eddying in from the north. Brand pointed at the great, cloud-draped mountain around and above them. Her eyes followed the gesture. A moment later so did her thoughts. It seemed incredible that thousands of miners had struck out from Skagway for the Klondlike gold fields, trudging on foot through two hundred inches of snow. Unbelievably, most of those desperate men and women had reached their goal. Were any of her fellow workers capable of duplicating that feat? Her answer came in a heartbeat. Brand. His eyes, his physical statement, the grit and determination bred into him told her that. The greater the challenge, the bolder he became. Kara took a deep, steadying breath.

What was she doing thinking such things?

"We have a little over three months to get the job done," Brand went on. "By then we'll be into winter. I've talked to each of you about the pace we'll be keeping, but I'm going to bring it up again. If anyone's having second thoughts, I want to know, now. I need to get the job done. My getting paid depends on that. At the same time, I'm not going to sacrifice anyone's safety. That's my number one concern. It always has been." He stopped, his gaze sliding over one worker after another. When he came to Kara, she squared to face him. Was it only her imagination that he seemed too slow to release her from his bold appraisal?

"I'm an EMT," he continued. "I've checked the town's medical clinic, and it can handle most emergencies. There's airlift to Juneau for anything serious. I hope none of that will be necessary." He paused. The ceaseless wind grabbed angrily at his black hair. He didn't bother trying to repair the damage. "There's something I only want to have to say once. This equipment costs more than I want to think about. Add to that the expense of shipping everything by ferry, and you have a pretty good idea of the bottom line. If I see anyone treating his equipment like junk, I'll tell him to draw his pay. Now, about your assignments . . .''

Ten minutes later Brand jumped down from his perch. Kara slapped her hardhat over her hair and breathed in the cleanest, sharpest air she'd ever tasted. Today she'd start earning her salary.

She wouldn't think about the impact on her senses caused by Brand's words, his hard, masculine body, the confrontation to come.

She wouldn't.

The morning was over before Kara had time to do more than pause for a swallow of coffee from her battered thermos. Although the temperature was in the low sixties, she'd been working hard enough that the braided hair trailing down her back felt heavy and uncomfortable. If she wasn't so used to it, she'd give in to impulse and whack it off.

Blasting had been done on the first switchback. Today she was responsible for pushing debris over the side. Her strong fingers gripped the levers, and her legs jabbed with practiced rhythm at the bulldozer's foot controls. Despite the activity around her, she felt isolated. Caught in the mesh of her thoughts.

She'd seen powerful men before. They were a fact of construction life. Despite their teasing and occasionally bold come-ons, she'd never felt as if she couldn't handle any situation. But something about Brand's presence . . . As an unexpected chill chased down her spine, she shivered. Sexy? Potent? Dangerous? Which was it? Maybe all three.

Certainly more than she wanted to deal with.

When the crew stopped for lunch, Kara climbed down out of the cab and carried her lunch box to a spot which gave her a view of the doll-like community far below. She could join the others, but her thoughts commanded too much of her attention for that. Maybe, if she'd been able to reach her family last night, she'd spend more time thinking about her father's reaction to her flight to Skagway, rather than her new boss.

Boss, she reminded herself firmly. That's all he was, nothing more. Once he understood her connection to the collapse in Anchorage, he might give her her walking papers, but he couldn't do more than that.

She lifted her hand, shielding her eyes against the sun that had just come out from behind a cloud. Far below, at one end of the town, she caught a glimpse of the creek, but the cabin she now called home was hidden among the trees. Still, thinking about last night helped settle her.

Although Kara hadn't wanted to impose, Ada had insisted she join them for dinner. Over coffee, she'd learned that only about seven hundred people lived in Skagway year around. Cliff and Ada knew all of them, their family histories, how they earned their livings, how much they made, whether they'd voted in the last election, whether they paid their electric bills. Now, looking down at tin roofs, gravel streets, and a sprinkling of trees, she was once again struck with a deep sense of respect for those who'd carved a community out of the wilderness.

Yesterday she'd told Brand she was interested in the area's history. This morning she meant it more than ever.

"It's hard to believe, isn't it?"

Kara turned. Brand stood over her. For a moment she struggled against the impulse to scramble to her feet in order to reduce the aura of size and strength surrounding him. Then she swallowed and pulled her emotions under control. He'd removed his flannel shirt. His t-shirt was frayed and spotted. What made the most impact was the way the snug garment revealed work-tempered muscles. She couldn't be sure whether he wore the jeans he'd had on yesterday. Maybe they all bonded to him in the same way. "What's hard to believe?" she managed, wrestling her unguarded thoughts into submission.

"That the town exists." He jammed his hands in his back pockets, looking, not at the distant town, but at her. "What you said earlier has gotten me to thinking about Skagway's origins. When I think of miners coming here knowing there were no grocery stores, no hospitals, no communication with the rest of the world, I'm in awe." He took a step closer and then, carefully, lowered himself onto a nearby rock. For a moment he said nothing, the silence between them feeling alive and electric. Kara sucked in oxygen, wanting to hear him speak again.

Afraid of her reaction to him.

He shook his head, his eyes on her, the valley below, her again. "Did those miners have any idea what they were getting into? I mean, they were businessmen, city folks. Gold fever must be an incredible thing. I think there's something to be learned from their courage."

Kara tried to concentrate on what he was saying, but her mind stayed on the way Brand favored his right leg. He was a mountain; mountains were supposed to be invincible. But he was also a human being. A man. Unnerved, she cast about for something to hinge a conversation on. "Cliff told me thirty men died working on the narrow-gauge railroad." She pointed toward the short length of track peeking through the trees a strong stone's throw away. This morning a train had passed by on it, holding her attention for as long as she could see it. "Looking at it, I can understand why."

"Cliff?"

"Cliff Bostian," she explained. "The man you told me to see about a place to stay."

"Then it worked out. It's going to be all right? I mean, it's what you were looking for?"

"That and more," she reassured him, surprised that it meant that much to him. "It's so private, sheltered."

"The way they described it, that's what I thought. Well, good."

She nodded, absently pushing at a strand of hair the wind had blown across her temple. Brand's eyes tracked the gesture, making her aware of her body in a way that felt new and untested. Conscious of their seclusion from the rest of the crew, she explained about the arrangement she and the Bostians had agreed to. "I'm hoping I can help, like replenishing their wood supply and replacing what passes for their bridge. That's going to be a big project, but it has to be done. Cliff can barely get around. Walking out to where they have to leave their truck is almost more than he can handle."

Brand frowned. "That's too bad. He didn't stand while I was talking to them. I got the impression he's pretty dependent on his wife."

"I think they're equally dependent, not that Ada would ever admit that. They snip at each other constantly, but it's clear they're in love. Those two—they're so much fun to be around. They're so proud of what they've done with their property. I'd never tell them it wouldn't make *House Beautiful*."

"I just hope they can stay there."

Brand's concern for the elderly couple left her feeling unsettled. He cared about people he'd only met once. And yet, he didn't care anything about a wonderful man who'd—*No. Don't. You don't know him.*

But, maybe if Brand understood who her father was—his stubborn and proud conviction that he knew best—Brand would understand why she'd come here and what she needed from him.

Maybe.

Brand opened his lunch box and took out a sandwich. He bit into it and chewed. For some reason the muscles in his jaw fascinated her. He spoke around cheese and bologna. "It sounds as if Cliff and Ada can tell you a lot about local history."

Taking Brand's lead, she focused on a conversation that revolved around Skagway. Brand had been here long enough to have picked up a little about the town's present-day activities. He told her about a summer theater that depicted the life of Skagway's most famous outlaw. Soapy, as he was called, was buried in the local cemetery, a popular attraction. A member of the volunteer fire department had suggested he check out the visitors' center, and, if he had time, a ride on the narrow-gauge would put the whole Klondike experience into perspective.

"I don't know when that's going to be." Brand took a final swallow of water from his thermos and closed his lunch box. "This job owns me. I don't know why I'm complaining. It's been like that for years." He shrugged. "I wouldn't know any other way to be."

Kara had already gotten to her feet when she noticed that Brand was having trouble standing. He started to put weight on his right leg, winced, then sat back down. Wordlessly, she held out her hand and waited for him to grip it. For a moment he locked eyes with her, and in their blue-black depths, she read frustration and surrender.

Then his hand engulfed hers. She leaned back, giving him something to brace against. As he pulled his feet under him, he sighed. "Thanks."

So slowly that she was aware of each finger drawing away from her, Brand put an end to the contact. He dropped his hand to his side and stared at hers. Uneasy, she spread her fingers over her thigh. Too late she realized she'd only drawn more attention to herself. He'd have to be blind not to realize the impact his touch had on her.

"You're all right?" she asked in an attempt to divert both him and herself.

"I will be."

"What happened?" *Dangerous question.*

"An accident. One that didn't have to be." His jaw tightened almost imperceptibly. If she hadn't been so focused on him, she would have missed it. "You said you came from Anchorage," he continued. "You must have heard about it."

She'd guessed right. The collapse had injured him. She felt half sick, facing the fact that the accident had exacted its toll on more than her brother. "The parking garage? Yes. Of course." She hated lying, evading. "I'd just finished a job on the Washington coast when it happened. In fact, I was going to be working on the project."

"You're lucky you weren't around when it went down."

"I guess I am," she said so softly she wasn't sure he could hear over the sound of a backhoe kicking to life. "Being up here makes learning what happened much harder."

"That matters to you?"

She swallowed, feeling trapped. *When he finds out the truth, he'll hate me for this moment.* "Of course it does. A structure doesn't just collapse."

Brand nodded and said something, but grinding gears drowned him out. He frowned and turned to watch the slowly moving backhoe. "No. It doesn't. And calling what happened an accident is a cop-out."

"What would you call it?"

"What? Negligence. Incompetence. Maybe greed."

For the better part of a minute, Kara stood where she was, feeling both trapped and angry. Not telling him who she was had preyed on her from the instant they met. A moment ago she'd felt like a diver poised over a dark, maybe bottomless pool. She might be terrified of catapulting herself into space, but at least the waiting would be over. She'd be honest. He'd react, and she'd know where she stood. Only, it hadn't happened. She was too much of a coward; she needed a job. Now work had taken him from her, and she had no choice but to climb down off that towering diving board and begin the process of waiting, thinking, anticipating all over again.

Don't look back, Brand chided himself as he headed toward his pickup. He wasn't at all sure Kara Richardson believed he'd sought her out simply because they shared an interest in history. If he gave away anything of what was going on inside him right now, it would be too much.

Why was he drawn to her? Grunting, Brand hoisted himself over a mound of rocks and dirt, answering his question almost as soon as it was asked. He'd have to be dead not to notice the femininity simmering beneath her practical clothes. That mass of hair. What would it look like flowing free over her shoulders? Feel like in his hands?

It might be just physical attraction; he couldn't deny that. But in the short time he'd known her, he'd sensed something else—common threads in their backgrounds, shared values, pride and competence.

She'd been married. Although she was still a stranger to him, he envied the man she'd allowed into the intimate circle of her thoughts and dreams. Whoever that man was, he'd been a fool for letting her go. A woman who could hold her own in this rough business the way she did had to be admired. She deserved a man who acknowledged and honored her competence.

Brand grunted again. What was he thinking, that he might fit that bill? Fat chance. She'd obviously been scraped raw by the divorce. That, he decided, was why she'd been so . . . unsettled . . . around him. What she needed was space and time, not her boss crowding that space. In three months she'd go back to where she'd come from, and he'd be on to his next job.

He'd forget her—except to ask himself if he'd ever find another woman capable of sharing his rugged world.

A hard, grinding noise pulled him out of his thoughts. He looked around, quickly locating the backhoe that had created the sound. Why couldn't some people understand the simple fact that, if a machine's gears were treated like junk, they wouldn't last. The first time he'd heard the complaining gears this morning, he'd tried to ignore the sound. The second time it happened, he'd glared at the man. Finally, he'd warned the driver to take it easy. Whatever the man muttered in return, he hadn't caught, but he didn't have to.

Fire him, Brand told himself. It wasn't as if the man didn't know where his boss stood. But reality intruded. Without the driver, he would be shorthanded. Besides, he hated canning someone who might have a family to support. He'd give him a final, clear warning. Hopefully the driver would straighten up his act. After all, only a fool would jeapardize the salary he was getting.

When his walkie-talkie squawked, Brand turned his attention from the backhoe. His foreman had a question about some reinforcing timbers that kept boulders from raining onto the road. A crew was ready to start digging into the hillside there, and the reinforcement wasn't needed any longer. Did Brand want the timbers dug or cut out? After telling his foreman he'd better take a look at the situation, he headed toward his pickup.

When he tried to step up into the high cab, his thigh protested. Swearing, he clamped a hand over his leg. He'd felt fine this morning, but six hours later, his thigh throbbed. If he insisted on subjecting it to this kind of punishment, it'd take longer than it should to heal.

And too often he'd need help standing, maybe from a woman with surprisingly soft hands and a slim silver ring circling her little finger. Brand maneuvered around the endless traffic snaking up and down the narrow road. Because he'd taken to the gravel on the side of the road, his 4-wheel drive bounced and banged, forcing him to grip the steering wheel to keep it on course. Yet, despite the need to concentrate, he felt, or thought he still felt, Kara Richardson's touch. Certainly he remembered the compassion in her eyes.

She hadn't fed him a line about being able to handle her job. Despite the care she gave her hands, she was stronger than she looked. And she operated her machinery as if she'd been born to the task. What was it she'd said? That she'd been doing construction work all her life. Not her adult life, her life.

They had that in common.

Deciding what to do with the sturdy wooden timbers wasn't hard. "There's no knowing how deep they go," Brand told his foreman as the two stood in the shade of the steep hillside. "Cut them off at the ground and put them aside."

"You want to hold onto them?"

"For a little while. We might have a use for them. How's it going? Does everyone look like they know what they're doing?"

Chuck Morse nodded and scratched under his armpit, then fired tobacco juice at a rock. "The Indian women don't need me telling them what to do. They're pros."

"That's the impression I got." Brand leaned his weight into one of the timbers sticking out of the ground. It didn't budge. "I didn't figure they'd be afraid of hard work. I just hope we can say the same about everyone."

"You sound as if you have reservations."

"Not really." Although slow-moving. Chuck had an instinct about the construction world that made him invaluable. In the past six years, the two men had gotten drunk together, worked through the night on more than one problem, weathered more governmental regulations and delays than he wanted to think about. Brand didn't know if Chuck called what they had a friendship. The word was something he had never tried to define. But he could be honest with Chuck and know the other man would keep a confidence. He told him about the backhoe operator.

"You don't need my advice, Brand. We both know this is a lean crew. But if he ruins something, you're going to be in worse trouble than if you're a worker short."

Chuck was right. Still, letting someone go had never been easy for him. If they did their jobs, his employees were well rewarded. But he had learned, the hard way, that if he got too close to one of his employees, and that person didn't perform his or her job, he wound up in the awkward position of calling someone he cared about to task. Holding back turned out to be easier all the way around. Isolating maybe, but he was used to that.

"I heard from her," Chuck said. "Sandy. She's coming up next week."

Brand glanced at Chuck's sweaty t-shirt. "I just hope you take a shower between now and then."

Chuck grinned, his forty-five-year-old face becoming ten years younger. "I might even wash my clothes. About our place, you don't think you could make yourself scarce for a couple of hours?"

"I might. If I was given the proper incentive."

"Incentive? You mean a bribe, don't you?"

Brand pretended to flinch. "We're discussing a business transaction. You're suggesting I put myself up at the hotel for the night. I'm sure not going to sleep in my truck. It's going to cost money."

"Give me a break. I'd do the same for you. That bulldozer operator sure isn't hard on the eyes. If the two of you hit it off . . ."

"You know how I feel about that."

"Yeah. I've heard you spouting off on the subject a time or two. The thing is, you aren't getting any younger. You've made your mark in this business. It doesn't own you. Everyone, you included, is entitled to a personal life.

Besides, if you don't wind up with some heirs, what's the point of amassing a fortune?"

Brand rolled his eyes. What fortune? "I think I've heard this before."

"Then listen for once. The only kind of woman who'd put up with you is one who understands this insane business."

Tired, battered, hungry, Kara turned off her bulldozer and climbed out of the cab. She took a few slow, careful steps while she waited for her body to adjust to the feel of quiet earth underfoot. Next to cleaning up and finding something to eat, only one thing was on her mind. Earlier, work had taken her toward the upper end of the project where she'd spotted a couple of treated timbers lying along the side of the road. They were long enough that they'd span the creek leading to Cliff and Ada's property. If he had no use for them, maybe Brand would let her throw them in the back of her pickup. Of course, she thought, as a backhoe jockeyed into position next to her bulldozer, she'd need help getting the timbers into her pickup, and building the bridge.

From who? Brand?

Darn! Instead of letting the engine idle before cutting it, the backhoe operator had stomped down on the gas. Diesel fumes filled the air and dark exhaust boiled out of the exhaust pipes. Kara backed away, trying not to breathe.

"What the hell are you doing?"

She started at the angry words, then realized they weren't aimed at her. She stood watching as Brand strode over to where the backhoe operator sat astride his machine. The backhoe's engine snarled and then died.

"I warned you about that earlier," Brand said, obviously not caring how far his voice traveled. "There's no call for the way you're treating it."

The backhoe operator jumped to the ground and turned to face Brand. The man was Brand's height but without his muscular build. "I don't have much choice, Lockwood," the operator shot back. "That beast's running so rough that punching it's the only way I can keep it from cutting out on me."

"I don't think so."

Although she was no stranger to rough male conversation, Kara felt a chill at Brand's words. In contrast to his earlier yelled warning, this was delivered with deadly calm.

"Are you saying I don't know my job?" the man asked.

"I'm saying if it's running rough, you work on it until it hums."

"I'm no mechanic."

Kara watched, both fascinated and uneasy, as Brand's facial muscles tightened, reminding her of the fierceness she'd found in him that first day. He had, she believed, what it took to stand up to everything life threw at him. "No mechanic?" He clipped the words. "I asked if you could work on machinery before I hired you. You assured me you could."

"You're calling me a liar?"

"No," Brand said, sounding weary. "I'm not calling you anything. Tomorrow morning, first thing, I want you to meet me at the trailer. I'll have your check ready."

Just like that. The speed with which Brand fired the man stunned Kara. Fighting the desire to wrap her arms around her middle and thus protect herself against the anger arcing from one man to another, she remained rooted to the spot as the fired worker took a step toward Brand, then whirled and stomped away.

She was trying to think of a way to fade into the background when a deep sigh, carried by the wind, reached her. Brand's face had undergone an incredible change. He looked years older than he had a few seconds ago. He ran his hand over his eyes, then shook his head, watching as the man he'd just fired jumped into his pickup. The pickup jerked forward, tires squealing.

Slowly Brand turned around. He blinked when he saw her. "I'm sorry," he said, his voice barely audible above the sound of the retreating vehicle. "That was supposed to be private."

"Sometimes that's not possible." She didn't move. When Brand closed most of the distance separating them, she straightened, determined not to reveal anything of what she felt. A minute ago she'd thought him hard-nosed, maybe even heartless. That was before his body language gave him away. Firing the man hadn't been easy for him.

"I think, out of everything I do, that's the hardest." Brand rammed his hands in his back pockets. "Does he have a family? I don't even know that about him."

"You could have asked him."

"Maybe." Brand looked as if he hadn't expected her to say that. "But that wouldn't have changed the outcome. He has his bottom line, bills to pay. So do I. Only my bottom line involves everyone on this mountain and a commitment I made to get a job done. If I don't deliver, no one gets paid." The wind blew his hair across his forehead. He yanked his hand out of his pocket and swiped. "How are you with backhoes?"

Brand had his bottom line. Now, right after he'd had to fire a man, wasn't the time to ask about the timbers. "I've operated my share of them."

"Give it a try tomorrow, will you? I'd like to know what you think about the engine. Maybe it does run rough."

"I don't think so," she admitted. "I heard it idling."

"You did?"

"Yes. You're not the only one who noticed how he handled it."

"Tell me something. If it was you, would you have let him go?"

Kara couldn't answer that. She didn't know what had gone on between Brand and the man before their confrontation. She explained that and listened while he told her about the previous warning.

"Then I would have done exactly what you just did," she told him.

He nodded then glanced around the mountain. "We're going to be the last two up here," he said, when for maybe the twentieth time that day clouds blew in to cloak the sky. "There's a microwave in the place Chuck and I rented, thank goodness. Otherwise, I'm not sure we'd bother with dinner. What are the cooking facilities like where you're staying?"

Kara admitted that she hadn't done any cooking on the old electric stove in her place yet. As the clouds built, Brand's eyes glided from deep blue into black, distracting her from everything except the power behind them. "I have to do some grocery shopping," she managed. "Ada said it'll cost me a fortune."

"I already found that out. Another time, I'd stock up before coming here." He shifted from one leg to the other. The movement triggered her memory of the difficulty he'd had getting to his feet after lunch, and his acceptance of her helping hand. Fingers tingling, she started toward her pickup and he fell in step beside her. She could ask him about the timbers. All he'd do was tell her he had another use for them.

But she didn't want to talk about rebuilding a bridge, or what either of them would have for dinner. Most of all she didn't want to think about saying the words that would drive a wedge between herself and this man.

She wanted to concentrate on the sound his boots made as he followed her to the flat area reserved for personal vehicles.

"I see you found transportation. It runs all right?" he asked when she reached to open her truck's door.

In a few words, she explained that she'd had to do some improvising in order to replace several worn hoses. She stared at her hand gripping the handle. In the two times they'd touched, he had to have noticed its diminutive size. Still, he didn't question her ability to make the truck operable. And, unless she'd read him wrong, he now believed her capable of doing the other work he'd hired her for. She'd passed his test; the knowledge filled her with pride.

Maybe more than pride.

Brand waited until she'd climbed into the cab and then rested his elbows on the open window. He'd probably shaved this morning, but his chin appeared hazed. If she touched him, which she wouldn't, her palm would feel scraped. Sensitized. She noticed that two of his knuckles were scratched. Had he ever had a woman touch her lips to his knuckles when they needed treatment? Wanted one to?

No. Don't think that way. They were employer and employee, and a word from her might end that.

"I hope you get to do that exploring you mentioned," he said. "The longer I'm here, the more I want to learn about the past."

"Do you?"

He nodded. "The narrow-gauge travels through the heart of White Pass trail where the miners were. You might want to take a ride—if your boss gives you the time off."

She grinned. "Maybe I'll have to play hookey." She knew she should put the key in the ignition and drive off so Brand wouldn't have to stand on his sore leg. But she didn't want to leave. What she wanted was to hear his answer if she suggested they ride the train together.

Not that she would.

THREE

"Kara. There'a a message for you."

All thoughts of Brand fled as Kara hurried into the house after Ada Bostian. She half remembered to smile at Cliff, who was seated in front of the TV confidently answering the questions being asked on a game show, then concentrated on the note Ada had scrawled on the back of an envelope. It didn't say much, just that her brother had called and wanted her to return the call as soon as possible.

"Did Hank say anything about our dad?" she asked.

"I'm afraid not. Your brother sounds like a nice young man. A little abrupt in his talking, but that's the way kids are these days, always in such a hurry."

She almost told Ada that Hank wasn't a kid, but she didn't take the time. Because there was only one phone in the house, there was nothing she could do about Ada and Cliff overhearing. What did it matter? If there was more trouble with their father . . .

Hank answered halfway through the second ring. "You just caught me," he explained through static. "I was on my way out the door."

52

"Why? Hank, what's up with Dad?"

"Are you sitting down?"

Don't ever say that! "Tell me. He's—he's all right, isn't he?"

"I don't know, sis. He's in the hospital."

Although she had to stretch the cord to reach a chair, Kara collapsed into it. Her head began pounding. "In the hospital," she repeated. *Why did I leave him?* "Oh no."

"Calm down," he said almost soothingly. "I don't think it's anything life threatening."

Life threatening? Not the man who raised me. She opened her mouth to ask for an explanation, but Hank was already a step ahead of her. In a calm voice that made her proud of her kid brother, he told her that Art Crayton had been off his feed for a couple of days and his color wasn't particularly good. Hank had chalked it up to worry about the accident, the investigation, his injuries, and Kara having to take a job in Skagway. "But halfway through getting ready to see his attorney earlier today, he passed out. Fortunately he was in the bedroom and landed on the bed. Still, it scared me. I called the ambulance."

The word ambulance made her lightheaded, but she waited Hank out. Apparently their father had come around before they reached the hospital and tried to order the attendants to take him back home, but because his vital signs didn't look too good, he'd been admitted. Tests were scheduled for tomorrow morning. In the meantime, their father was making the nurses wish he'd pack up and leave. "I see where he's coming from," Hank said. "It's making me more patient than I thought I'd be, given the way he won't let up about how I wasted money on an ambulance."

"He's being rough on you?"

"Not really. I pretend like I don't hear him when he gets going on that. He's just got so much on his mind that it makes him edgy. The last thing he wants to do is deal with health problems. Besides, you know how he is about maintaining his macho image.''

''Yes. I do know. What do you think it is? I mean, you're around him. You probably know more about him than the doctors do.'' *More than I do right now.*

''Stress,'' Hank said without missing a beat. ''One minute he's raving about how slow the investigation's going; the next I can't get him to say a word. You know what he's like; if anything he's kicked it into a higher gear since you left. He can't sit still, forgets to eat, can't sleep. By the way, he has a message for you.''

''He does?'' She wasn't sure she wanted to hear this.

''Yeah. Our father lovingly said that if he could get his hands on you, he'd wring your neck. His exact words were, 'if I'd known she was going to work for Lockwood, I would have nailed her foot to the floor.' ''

''I didn't have a choice; he didn't give me one.''

''You and I know that, but he feels betrayed. Look at it from his point of view. You left him a note letting him know where you were going instead of telling him face to face.''

Because I couldn't stand seeing the look in his eyes. ''Did you tell him we need the money?''

''Twice, at least. He doesn't want to talk about that part. He believes you've gone behind his back.''

''Did you tell him he left me no choice?''

''I didn't have to. Your note spelled that out.''

''Hank? I'm sorry all this was dumped on you. Do you want me there?''

''Not now. If something else happens, maybe.''

''Are you sure?''

''Sure. I'm not a kid you know. Besides—'' For a few seconds static cut Hank off. ''Can you hear me? I was just going to say, we already agreed that, because of the way Dad's clammed up, the only way we're going to get all the facts is by talking to everyone who was there. Especially Lockwood.''

"That's what I told Dad, in the note.''

"I know. Look, just before he took his dive, he was saying he doesn't want you saying anything to Lockwood until he's had a chance to talk to you. That's the first thing he said when he came to. It's really got him upset. He made me promise I'd ask you to hold off a few days until you and he can talk. You haven't told Lockwood, have you? I figured if you had, you'd be hitching a ride back by now.''

"No. The timing—it's not the easist thing to bring up.'' Kara glanced at Ada and Cliff who were staring at the TV—now a soft drink ad. She needed to tell Hank more but that would have to wait until they had privacy.

"Good.'' The word came out in a whoosh of air that reached across the miles. "I'm sure Dad's realized you wouldn't be where you are if he'd confided in us. Maybe he's decided it's time to stop treating us like children. You've taken matters into your hands; he can't get away with the silent treatment any more. Only, if you can, give him a little time to work out what he needs to say.''

"All right,'' she said softly. "I want—you know I want things to be right between us. Hank? Tell Dad I love him. Maybe I should try to reach him at the hospital.''

"Wait until tomorrow. They've given him something so he'll sleep. Brother, can that man snore.''

Kara asked Hank how he was doing and then, although she didn't want to lose contact with her brother, she let him go. When she turned from the phone, she wasn't surprised to see Ada and Cliff looking at her. Ada asked if there was anything they could do, her eyes dark with concern.

"No. Thank you,'' she said around the knot in her throat. "My father isn't feeling too well, but it doesn't sound like anything critical.'' She took a calming breath.

"It's just that it's hard to hear this when I'm so far from him."

"Of course it is, my dear." Ada pushed herself to her feet and patted Kara on the shoulder. "How about some hot chocolate? Maybe that'll make you feel better."

Kara wasn't sure hot chocolate would solve many problems. Still, Ada's gesture was so sweet. Besides, she wasn't ready to be alone with her thoughts.

By the next morning, Kara had reconciled herself to the fact that it might be several days before she knew anything definite about her father's health. She'd tried to talk to him first thing, but he'd sounded so dopey that she wasn't sure he'd remember the call.

Only one thing he said made sense: he wanted her word that she'd wait to talk to Brand Lockwood. "Do this for me, honey," he'd said, his voice groggy. "Please. For my sake."

Now, listening as Brand outlined the day's work, she couldn't help wondering what the consequences of keeping her promise to her father might be. Brand told the crew that they were now one man short, and he had no alternative except to ask the others to take up the slack. "I'd just as soon not have to rehash my reasons for firing him. Let's just say that his attitude jeopardized the entire project. I will not let that happen. I can't."

His words rang through Kara, reminding her, as if she needed reminding, of his code of ethics. He hated irresponsibility; he would hate a liar even more. In the short time she'd known him, she'd come to respect and admire Brand Lockwood. When he could no longer feel the same about her, it would hurt.

She'd started toward her machine when Brand overtook her. She turned toward him, all too aware of him. "I haven't heard anyone disagree with the action I took," he told her. "Apparently you weren't the only one who thought I had a problem employee." He smiled. "Well, you've had another night to sleep in it. Do you still feel the same about the cabin? It didn't fall down around your ears?"

"Not yet," she assured him, determined not to let him know how uneasy her night had been, how uneasy she still felt. "But that roof's not going to last another winter. I swear, I can see the stars through the seams. I can just see me in a storm running around putting pans under all the leaks."

"Hm. I don't imagine it's easy for the Bostians, admitting they can't do the work they used to."

"I'm sure it isn't."

Brand nodded. "But your living arrangements are going to work out? There's nothing critical you can't live with?"

She described the condition of the bridge in detail. "I'm sorry. You already know it isn't passable. It's just that I'd like to help."

"I'm sure you would. Maybe, if we put our heads together, we can come up with something. If someone had to get to them in a hurry, they can't be worrying the bridge might collapse."

She agreed, struck by the note of genuine concern in Brand's voice. He cared about an elderly couple he barely knew. And yet he might be instrumental in destroying her father's career. She wanted to hate him for that, but things, life, was much too complicated for that simple emotion. After a few seconds during which her mind went in directions she barely comprehended, she mentioned that she wanted to talk to Ada and Cliff about more of the things that needed doing but wasn't quite sure how to bring that up. "I want to be sensitive to their pride. Not have them think I see them as helpless."

Brand nodded, then, although she didn't need help, he indicated he would assist her into the bulldozer's cab. She reached for the handhold, trying not to think about his hands around her waist. It didn't work. Brand Lockwood had made his impact on her, body and mind.

The moment Brand saw the homemade bridge, he knew Kara hadn't exaggerated its condition. He wasn't sure he wanted to walk across it, let alone drive a vehicle over it. Especially not a four wheel drive weighed down with timbers, he thought as he jockeyed his pickup into place. It had taken three men to hoist the timbers onto the truck bed after work. Now, with the help of a crowbar for leverage, he managed to drop the heavy logs onto the ground.

Then, although he was hungry and dirty and tired, he walked across the bridge and down the narrow road. He heard a dog barking, the sound muffled as if it was inside. Certainly whoever was home would know they had company. He owed them the courtesy of letting them know what he was up to.

Maybe he should have told Kara what he had in mind, but she'd taken off as soon as work was over, her truck bouncing down the road as she took the turns as fast as she could. Why? Because she was expecting a call from someone—her ex-husband? Maybe another man. A beautiful, intelligent, competent woman like Kara Richardson wouldn't be without a man in her life, would she?

What did he care?

As he broke through the alders and reached the small opening, he understood the area's appeal. If a person wanted privacy, this was the place for it. His attention was drawn first to the main house with its less than level porch and then to what he could see of the little cabin behind it. So that was where Kara was staying.

Although he wanted to go to the cabin, he headed toward the house. But before he could start up the stairs, the cabin door opened. He waited, content to do nothing but watch Kara's slow emergence from the shadows. Her feet made no sound on the packed earth; she moved smoothly, easily, totally in control of her body. By the time she'd come close enough that they could carry on a conversation, he'd become aware of two things—only two things. She'd just washed her hair; it hung soft and dark and shining around her shoulders, draping nearly to her waist. And she wore, not jeans and a practical shirt, but a loose shift of some kind that ended at her knees. So she had legs, slender, strong, beautiful legs.

A bulldozer operator? No. She was more, much more than that.

If she'd been surprised to see him here, she'd had time to recover while her features were still hidden from him. "What was that I heard?" she asked. She pulled her hair away from her neck, the gesture both graceful and sensual. "It sounded like something heavy hitting the ground."

He explained about the timbers, feeling not at all like the confident, competent owner of a construction company. She'd slipped into sandals. They made her look even more feminine. He could smell whatever she'd used to shampoo her hair with, a light, clean scent that drifted around him. She wore a single piece of jewelry; the small cameo necklace settled comfortably against her throat.

This woman shouldn't be building a road. She should . . . should what?

"I've come at a bad time," he said.

"Oh, no. I'm sure Cliff and Ada will be delighted to see you. They're probably watching us right now."

"Not for them. For you." Had he really said that?

"Oh." She looked down at her legs, ran her long fingers through her hair to squeeze more moisture from it. He felt his body temperature rise a half dozen degrees. "Ada put a new heating element in the water heater today," she explained. "When she told me that, I *had* to try out the shower."

He should say something about her landlords, give her the impression that he wasn't at all affected by the way she was dressed, smelled, looked. Still, when he tried to come up with something, he drew a blank. Fortunately, a loud squeak filled the silence. He turned to see Ada standing by the front door, a frown on her face as she glared at the door hinge. Then she peered at him and a grin spread over her face. "Mr. Lockwood. What are you doing here?"

For the second time in only a few minutes, he explained that he wanted to see if some excess timbers might be put to good use. "It looks as if they're going to work. They're certainly long enough to span the creek."

Ada clasped her hand over her chest and sighed dramatically. "See what living right will get you, Kara. Of course—" She winked. "There's just the slightest possibility that that old wreck of a bridge isn't the only reason Mr. Lockwood came here. Well?"

Well, what, Brand wanted to ask. But before he could, Kara explained that she'd offered to help Ada with dinner and had been on her way to their place when he arrived. Feeling like an outsider, he said he didn't want to hold anyone up and turned to leave.

"Don't you dare." Ada planted her hands on her considerable hips. "How can you even think I'd let you go without extending my hospitality? We do have enough of that stir fry stuff for another mouth, don't we?"

"Of course." Kara didn't sound thrilled. And although he wondered if she hoped he'd turn down the invitation, he didn't. Why should he? he wondered as they stepped inside. After all, he had done the Bostians a good deed. A home-cooked meal seemed like a fair trade, especially one prepared by an attractive woman wearing a garment that slipped and slid over her slender body.

He hoped he'd been wrong about her hurrying home because of a man. And he wished to hell he could remember what he'd always said about not mixing his business and personal life.

As soon as Cliff heard what Brand had done, the older man started talking about what would be the best way to build a bridge that would last. As he drank a beer and watched Kara move about in the kitchen, Brand offered a few suggestions, but for the most part he agreed with what Cliff had in mind. The truth was, at this moment, bridge construction was the last thing on his mind. When, Cliff asked, would Brand be able to get some men here to do the work? Ada chided her husband. Mr. Lockwood— Brand—was doing this out of the goodness of his heart. Cliff had no call to be pressing him.

"You get off my back, old woman," Cliff shot at his wife. "My body might have gone bad on me, but there's nothing wrong with my mind. Or my mouth." Grinning, he winked at Brand. "Brand and I can settle this man to man, without your interference."

"This isn't interference," Ada snapped. "You get your tongue to wagging, and it doesn't know when to stop."

"Can you blame it? With you yacking away, I get little enough chance to talk. You ever try stir fry?" he asked Brand. "These women here, they've been trying to tell me that it's good for me. But I figure if I can't tell the meat from the rest of that stuff, someone's trying to hide something. I just hope you don't try to poison me."

Kara glanced over her shoulder at Brand, grinned, then rolled her eyes skyward. Brand bit down on his lower lip to keep from laughing. After a moment he explained that he thought he'd be able to get enough volunteers here on Sunday, but since that was their one day off work, they might not show up at the crack of dawn.

"Fine. Fine. Old woman, we'd better stock up on beer. Bridge building works up a powerful thirst."

Once again Kara shot Brand a quick smile. He held onto the memory of that gesture all through dinner, trying to tell himself that she was quiet simply because Cliff and Ada were doing so much talking—arguing—that it was impossible for her to get a word in. Still, he couldn't ignore the sense that she wasn't entirely comfortable in his presence. He could come up with a half dozen reasons for her to feel that way, none of which made him feel good.

Not long after dinner was over, Brand announced that he'd better get home. It wasn't that he didn't want to be around Kara, but if she was barely going to acknowledge his presence, he wouldn't draw out the evening. "That really was a good meal," he said for the third time. "I guess it's time I learned there's more to food than meat and potatoes. Well—"

Ada clamped her hand over his shoulder, holding him to the couch. "You can't."

"Can't?"

"Leave. I promised Kara I'd show her some of the pictures we've taken of Skagway over the years. I want you to see them, too."

He looked at Kara, but she didn't meet his gaze. He almost asked for a rain check, then changed his mind. He hadn't seen his parents for months. There was something about the words Cliff and Ada used, their way of handling themselves, their ease in each other's presence, that made him want to draw out the evening. "I'd like that," he said and settled back on the couch.

Although neither Cliff nor Ada were professional photographers, the pictures they'd taken told a vivid story of how the town had changed from a sleepy, isolated community to one that managed to both entice tourists and retain a basic honesty. There were pictures of gold-era buildings being remodeled, the evolution of the visitors' center and fish hatcheries, the ways the seasons painted the landscape. Brand listened, fascinated as Cliff brought the Klondike gold rush era to life with finely drawn stories of the men and women who settled the area. When he glanced over at Kara, he saw that she was leaning forward, her eyes alight with interest. Good. They shared a common interest.

"It's incredible," she said in an awe-filled voice. "To think that miners were willing to travel over 600 miles to reach the gold fields. I wonder how many people alive today would have the courage for that."

"I don't know." Brand shifted position on the couch he shared with Kara. She was better than a foot away. Still, he was as aware of her as if they'd been touching. He could still smell her hair's clean scent. He swallowed and went on. "What amazes me is that the miners, many of whom had grown up in cities, struck off knowing there was nothing except wilderness ahead of them. No communication system, no rescue operations."

Kara sighed. "They were brave, and desperate. That's what really gets to me, how badly they needed money and the risks they were willing to take. A lot of them didn't have any other way of supporting themselves. That and simple gold fever. I've been thinking. I'd like to see Chilkoot Summit. Maybe that's the only way I'll really understand what it was like to pack a year's worth of supplies over a mountain."

"I've been up it," Ada offered. "When my legs were a lot stronger. I still don't believe it."

Cliff interrupted his wife to point out that neither of them had ever had any interest in attempting the climb in the winter like the miners. Anyone who would willingly tromp through as much as 200 inches of snow had marbles for brains. Although Brand felt his blood race at the prospect of such an adventure, he had to admit Cliff had a point. "There's still gold around, isn't there?"

"Plenty. Only, it's damn hard to pull out and once you do, you're not going to get paid enough to make it worthwhile these days. I guess, if you've got nothing better to do, it's something you can tell your grandchildren about. Me, I've got better things to do with my time."

Brand sensed Kara's eyes on him. When he met her gaze, he knew what she was thinking. Cliff's days were filled with staying warm and comfortable, excelling at game shows, and giving his wife a hard time—worthy pursuits for a man who'd been around almost eighty years.

He wanted her to know about the most important man in his life, tell her that although his father was retired, Steven Lockwood still talked as if he regularly punched a time clock and would resent it if anyone so much as hinted that he should be spending time in a rocking chair. He'd explain about his mother's passion for roses, her volunteer work in the schools.

And Kara would tell him about her family. What, he wondered, did her parents think of what she was doing and where she'd come to live.

Then Kara yawned and he realized he was so tired himself that just the thought of having to drive home and get ready for tomorrow made him shudder. Although Ada and Cliff were still arguing over how long it took to hike the Chilkoot trail, he pushed himself to his feet and started for the door.

"Don't you be rushing off," Ada said, her voice loud enough to jar his senses. "We've just started going through our pictures."

"Maybe another time. I've got to get up early."

"You're right. And so does she." Ada indicated Kara. "Why don't you walk her back to her place, make sure she gets home safe?"

Brand watched, curious to see how Kara would react to Ada's blatant attempt at keeping them together. Kara pointed out that the only danger she'd be in while going home would be if she tripped over someone named Mooch who apparently was off prowling somewhere tonight. Undaunted, Ada said she was uneasy about the stovepipe in the cabin and would Brand mind taking a look at it. Although he'd never considered himself an expert on stove-pipes, Brand didn't tell Ada that.

"They're characters," he said as they headed toward the cabin. "Are you sure you're up to a summer of this?"

"They're fine. Fine."

"I know they are. If you don't want to retain me to advise you on your stove, just say the word."

Kara reached for the cabin door, then turned toward him. "No. That's all right. This was a little ridiculous, though. I need to go back there to make a phone call in a little while."

To your ex? To a boyfriend? "And then you can go to bed?"

"Yes. Well, what do you think?" She stepped inside, snapped on a light, and pointed. Brand entered, determined to look only where she'd indicated. But the small room smelled as if she'd just taken her shower; he couldn't shake himself free. The cabin had been built from whole logs, with most of it covered with plasterboard, a strange setting for someone who looked as fragile as Kara did at this moment. At the far end stood the small potbellied stove. One wall was almost completely taken up with a sagging old couch covered by a wool blanket. There were three large calenders taped to another wall, all from the 1980s with pictures of grizzly bears. There weren't any curtains for the windows, just old sheets. Threadbare throw rugs covered the hardwood floor.

"It's even more rugged than I expected," he said. He took another breath. The place still smelled of nothing except her.

She stopped halfway to the stove. "I won't argue that. Does it look like a crusty old bachelor's pad?"

"It looks like it needs help," he came up with. During another look around, he noticed that the ceiling had been "finished" in sagging drywall. That made him concerned that the wood stove wouldn't pass any kind of building code. But after tapping on the lengths of pipe, he determined that at least here quality hadn't been compromised. "It's not the straightest pipe I've ever seen, but it looks sturdy enough."

"That's what I decided—while I was cleaning the pipe last night."

He turned, surprised to see a faint smile touching her lips. She didn't say anything, only stood there still looking like someone who should indulge herself in bubble baths, lace underwear, the finest of perfumes. He guessed what had made her smile, that she knew Ada only wanted to get them together. But Kara didn't say anything, and he didn't either. There was an adequate supply of wood near the stove, but because he guessed she'd placed it there, he also guessed that she didn't need him to play master fire builder.

Tonight she might look like someone who needed protecting, pampering, but she wasn't.

"Well . . ." He took a step toward the door, then stopped. He wanted to tell her to put on jeans and boots so he could think straight. He also wanted to let her know how beautiful she looked tonight. But he couldn't, wouldn't. He was her boss, and she had a life that didn't include him, like that phone call. "Well, I'd better be going."

She lifted her hand and touched her throat. His attention was drawn to her smooth flesh, the slender neck. He felt her gaze harden and knew she'd caught him at it. "I was admiring your necklace," he blurted. "It looks old."

She fingered the tiny oval, eyes still cautious, not quite believing. "It was my mother's."

"She gave it to you?"

"I put it on when she died. I was eight. I've always worn it."

Although he was so tired that he had to work to keep from yawning, he wasn't immune to the emotion behind the words. "Eight. That's a hard time for a girl to lose her mother."

"Yes." She whispered the word. "I wish . . ."

You wish she was still here. "I'm sorry. You were raised by relatives?"

"By my father." Her whisper became even fainter, hesitant even. "He took care of me and my younger brother. I was—he's a good parent." She'd been looking at the ground. Now her head came up and she met his gaze, her eyes suddenly fierce. "Stubborn and proud and independent but a good man."

"I'm sure he is." Why was she defending her father to him?

"He wasn't too strict. He always did the best he could."

"I'm sure he did." When she didn't say anything, he felt trapped by the silence. In an effort to get the conversation going again, he told her that his parents were retired from their government jobs and now spent their time renovating old houses in Seattle—among other things. "My dad handled contracts for federal buildings. I went with him to a construction site when I was five or six. One look at all that machinery and I was hooked. I told my folks that's what I wanted to do with my life—drive a tractor."

"Oh."

Oh? Couldn't she come up with more than that? When she continued to stare at him, her fingers worrying the slender chain at her throat, his mind went blank and his body hot. All he knew was that he'd fall asleep thinking about what she was doing, how she looked standing with her weight on her right hip, her now dry hair gently framing her features. And her legs. He'd think about her legs.

"Well . . ." Hadn't he already said that? "I'll see you tomorrow."

"Fine. Fine."

* * *

Fine? Kara winced as her final words to Brand echoed through her. Hopefully he'd chalk her less than intelligent conversation up to exhaustion. Even more hopefully, he'd have better things to think about than her.

Only, she didn't think so. The way he'd looked at her, eyes darkening, told her differently.

How much had she said about her father? Enough to make him suspicious?

No, of course not.

Maybe not.

After arguing with herself for a few more minutes, Kara walked back over to the Bostian's house to make her phone call. When she tried to reach her father right after work, she learned he'd been released from the hospital and had left word for her that he and Hank were going out to dinner but would be home later. She'd been nervous he might try to reach her while Brand was there. He hadn't. Instead, he informed her after he picked up the phone, he and Hank had just gotten back after driving by the construction site.

"They haven't started cleaning up a thing. It's all still sitting there looking—you know."

She did. She'd seen. "They must not be done with the on-site investigation," she offered. "Do you think they'll want your crew to do the clean-up?" Because Ada and Cliff had wandered off to look at the timbers Brand had delivered, she felt free to talk.

"What do you think?" Her father snorted. "They're not going to want me anywhere around."

Hoping to give him something else to think about, she asked if there'd been any good-looking nurses at the hospital. Her attempt fell flat. All her father wanted to talk about was how much the bill would be and whether his insurance might balk at paying.

"What did you find out?" she asked. "Did the doctor say your problem was stress related?"

"He said I'm getting old."

"He must have said more than that. What's his number, Dad? I'll call—"

"If you were here, you would have already talked to him."

Kara took a deep breath, trying to calm herself. He had a right to speak his mind—just as she had a right to do what she believed she had to.

"It's good money, Dad. We need it."

"I know that." Suddenly he sounded old and tired. "But Lockwood . . ."

"You know why."

For a minute she heard nothing except her father's ragged breathing. "I feel like my daughter's going behind my back."

"Only because you won't tell me anything," she said gently. She waited a minute, hoping he'd decide to end his stubborn, proud refusal to involve her in *his* problem. "I know Brand Lockwood was on the site that day and that he'd come there to talk to you about certain details of the construction," she pressed when he remained silent.

"He had no business, no right."

The building collapsed, Dad. "What did he say to you? Can't you at least tell me that?"

Silence. Still, Kara wasn't surprised. That had been her father's reaction when she asked the same question not long after the accident. Whatever passed between her father and Brand wasn't something Art Crayton wanted to share with his daughter. But the answer might prepare her for the result of the investigation. Surely he knew that.

"Dad, I'm not a child. I can handle the truth."

"The truth?"

She took a deep breath, aware of what her father was trying to do. But if he thought he could get her to back away from what she believed she had a right to know, he was wrong. "Lockwood talked to the investigators, Dad. Maybe that's why they're doing such a thorough job. Maybe he told them things they can't ignore."

"That's what you think, is it?"

An outsider might sense an irreparable rift between father and daughter, but she knew different. Her father had never backed down from a challenge, even if it was issued by her. "An awful lot points to that. If you won't tell me why Lockwood was there and what he said to you and how you felt—"

"Don't."

Kara closed her eyes, concentrating. "Don't what?"

"Don't ask questions. Please. Not of me, and not of him."

Please? Her father never said please.

"Kara?" he said after a minute of silence. "Are you still there?"

"Yes." *Dad, what's going on?*

"I just wish you would trust me."

I wish I could, too. How I want that. "Dad, I want to defend you, but how can I if I don't know anything? Why can't you trust *me*?"

"I'll take care of it. I always have, haven't I? I just want you to come home."

"I can't." She spoke around a flood of emotion. Didn't he know there was nothing she would rather do? "Someone in this family has to be bringing in money. Hank's hurt and you . . ."

"And no one will give me a job. Honey, please, don't talk to him. Don't tell him who you are."

"Why not?"

"Because—for my sake, don't. Please."

Please. There was that word again. "Do you know what you're doing to me?"

"All I know is that my life's blown up in my face. I have to have my daughter on my side. Don't you understand that?"

"Yes. Of course I do."

"I hope to God you do."

FOUR

What was wrong with her father? High blood pressure? Did a person pass out from high blood pressure?

What about his heart?

Kara leaned to the left, stuck her head out of the bulldozer cab, and sucked in a deep breath of air. She immediately began coughing, realizing too late that she was working in the fumes of a backhoe so close that she could nearly shake hands with the operator. A constant stream of vehicles plowed past, their presence seriously reducing her work space. She jockeyed her machine around as best she could and went back to work, smoothing a great mound of gravel over a drain pipe that extended out over a dropoff.

Why had her father begged her to say nothing? Why had she agreed? That was the insanity of it; she'd agreed.

Well, she'd have to call him back and tell him she couldn't go on deceiving Brand. But maybe—she shoved on a lever, feeling the machine strain—maybe she should wait until—until what?

She shoved again. When the bulldozer continued to act as if it was miring down, she backed up as far as she dared on the narrow ledge between blacktop and nothing, then started forward again, thinking to approach the small gravel mountain from a slightly different angle.

What did you accuse my dad of? The words weren't that hard. Why did her stomach tie itself into knots every time she thought about saying them to Brand? Why—

Darn! If whoever had deposited the gravel hadn't placed it so close to the drop-off, she wouldn't feel as if she was attempting a high wire act with an awkward, multi-ton partner.

Concentrating now, she gripped the steering lever and yanked on it. One way or other she'd complete her assignment and get her equipment back on stable ground. Then she'd have a serious talk with the person who had left the gravel there. She might be a skilled operator, but bulldozers weren't made for balancing acts. She absolutely *had* to have more space in which to work.

"Look out!"

The deep yell slammed at Kara's senses, but she didn't dare take her mind off what was happening long enough to acknowledge it. Before she had time to do anything except tense, she felt the bulldozer lurch to the left and begin sliding. Sliding! She stared, seeing nothing but air— miles of air.

"Bail out!"

Right! But if she did that, the bulldozer would careen off the side of the mountain. Not yet. Think! Damn it, think!

Praying, teeth grinding, she slammed her foot down on the brake pedal and hauled back on the steering lever. Slowly, too slowly, the bulldozer fought to respond. It was tilted so sharply now that she could barely stay in her seat. She leaned in the opposite direction, working carefully now, heart thudding. She felt the track skid, and she held on so tightly she tore a nail and then prayed.

Then, at what had to be the last possible second, the

track bit into earth and rocks and ground out a protest. She held on with sweat-slickened fingers, willing the bulldozer to obey her command, while the massive piece of equipment slowly crawled back up the steep slope. She counted its progress in inches.

It teetered on the edge of the road; then, when she raised the bucket to change the center of gravity, the monster clawed itself the last previous two feet.

Thank God.

She leaned forward, breathing deeply, staring at the mountain ahead of her—a mountain back where it should be. She felt both hot and cold, sick to her stomach. Proud of herself for having accomplished the impossible.

"Kara? What happened?"

Looking down at Brand, she could only wait until she trusted her voice. "I'm not sure."

"Not sure? What the hell are you talking about?"

"I had a little on my mind," she snapped. Raw nerves and pain from her torn nail drove the words. "Like staying alive and saving your stupid equipment. I'm sorry if I didn't take a picture for you."

She expected Brand to say something. Instead, he only stared up at her from under his hard hat, his eyes all but burning a hole in hers. He'd clenched his jaw and made fists of his hands. He looked as if he'd been punched.

Although he continued to gaze at her in that dark, intense way of his, she shook herself free long enough to test the engine and levers. Everything seemed to be in working order, something she wasn't sure she could say about herself. Because most of the other workers were staring at her, she couldn't guess which one had called out a warning.

"Get down."

Brand had barely spoken loudly enough to be heard over the sound of machinery, but his tone was all she needed. After turning off the engine, she jumped down out of the cab and faced her boss. She was trembling. For an instant a frightening question assaulted her. Had it been her fault? Because she'd been thinking about her father, she'd almost lost her boss hundreds of thousands of dollars worth of equipment and jeopardized her life? No. She'd never allowed herself to be seriously distracted while on the job.

"It won't happen again."

He went on glaring at her, his eyes continuing to dig.

"I mean it, it won't happen again."

"I hope to hell not."

She'd had all she could take of his temper. She was the one who'd almost lost her life. But she hadn't. Except for doing serious damage to her nervous system and a forefinger, there'd been no harm done.

She took a deep breath, grateful for the cool breeze that skittered over her, slowing her pulse. "I didn't have enough space in which to maneuver. I'm not offering that as an excuse, but if I see a situation like that again, I'll change it, not try to work in it."

"Will you?"

"Yes." She glared at him. "Believe me, yes. Look Brand, we both know this is a dangerous business. There are going to be near accidents, problems. It's a fact of life."

"I know that. Only, years ago I made myself a vow. That no employee of mine would ever be killed. You damn near made a liar out of me just now."

"Give it a rest, Lockwood. It's not the crime of the century; there wasn't a crime this time."

Both Kara and Brand started at the unexpected words. When she turned in that direction, she saw Brand's foreman, Chuck Morse, walking toward them. "I saw," Chuck said. "The bank gave way. She couldn't foresee that."

"Couldn't she?"

"No. She couldn't. She handled the situation like a pro.

Knowing her machine's center of balance and knowing how to make that work is what saved things. Give her the credit she deserves.''

The bank gave way. She'd suspected as much. "It's your decision, Lockwood," she told the big, dark man who'd complicated her world in ways he couldn't possibly comprehend. "If you feel I've done something you can't live with, give me my walking papers. I'd rather hear it straight out that you don't want to work with me."

"Walking papers?"

"You'll be even shorter handed than you are now, but if you feel you can't trust me—"

"Don't put words in my mouth, Richardson. I didn't say that."

She gave him a probing look and ignored her still hammering heart. "It sounds like it."

"If you weren't so damn defensive, you'd hear what I'm saying." He blinked and paused as if hearing himself for the first time. "Look at it from my point of view, will you? I'm responsible for the safety of everyone here. When that's jeopardized by anyone, I take it seriously."

"I know you do. Believe me, I know. Only, I didn't jeopardize anything except my own life by trying to save the 'dozer." *Stop it. You're treading on dangerous ground.* She swiped the back of her hand over her forehead, pushing her hair back where it belonged. Her scalp felt damp. "What if we both admit we flew off the handle? We can either spend the rest of the day hashing this over or get back to work."

To her surprise, a look of respect crept into his eyes. With his hands still hooked in his pockets, he regarded her for several seconds, then nodded. "You're up to it? You don't need to take a breather?"

By way of answer, she hoisted herself into the cab. Now that she'd distanced herself from him, it should be easier to think, shouldn't it? "I fell off a horse," she explained. "I'm getting back on it. End of discussion."

"Not quite." As she watched, Brand stepped onto the push arm and, holding onto the canopy side, stared in at her. "You're tough. I need that in an employee. But don't ever let toughness stand between you and emotion. You're bound to feel some backlash from what almost happened. Don't pretend you don't."

"I'm not pretending anything, Brand." She held up her hand to let him see that it was still trembling. "And if you think I can turn off emotion, you don't know me."

"I can't read minds, Kara. Sometimes I wish I could. The only way I'm going to know what goes on inside you is if you tell me."

Three days after the incident with the bulldozer, Kara received news that both eased her mind about those she'd left behind and gave her even more to concern herself with.

"Dad's not home yet, so I'm free to talk," her brother informed her when she reached him after work on a windy, overcast day. "How about you?"

According to the note that had been tacked to their door, the Bostians were off visiting friends and wouldn't be back until late. "I have the place to myself. How's it been going with Dad? Every time I try to talk to him about his health, he clams up."

"Tell me about it. I managed to have a brief meeting with his doctor yesterday. I learned that our old goat of a parent checked himself out of the hospital before all the tests had been taken. Of course, he didn't bother telling us that because he knew how we'd react. However, and that's why I'm glad you called, judging by what the doctor has seen, there's nothing major."

Kara closed her eyes, feeling damp heat behind her lids. How she loved that maddening old goat! "I hope the doctor's right. Hank, if I flew down for a day or so, do you think it'd make a difference? I mean, do you think I could sweet talk him into finishing the tests?''

"Not a chance. He gets red in the face every time your name comes up these days. It really gets to him that he can't run the show the way he did when we were kids. You and I have already talked about this, but it's true. He doesn't know how to handle not being in charge of his life, his future. I think it takes him back to when Mom died.''

"I know it does. That's why I'm doing this, trying to help despite him. He's really angry at me?''

"Not really. He loves you too much for that. But he's afraid you're going to learn something he doesn't want learned. He can't stop you. That has him off balance. Everything has him off balance. You haven't asked where he is.''

No. She hadn't. When she did, she learned that Art Crayton had been hired to do some consulting work for a private firm that wanted to pick his brain and didn't care about his present problems. "It's only part time, but it gets him out of the house. It helps his ego, and believe me, right now he needs the boost.''

"Oh, I know he does. That's why I wish he'd confide in us instead of thinking he can tough it out alone. What do you mean, right now? Has something else happened?''

Hank explained that he'd just learned that a structural diagnostician had been sent in to look at the wreckage. "A structural diagnostician? They didn't even have such things when Dad got going in the business. You remember Dave Rayburn? I went to school with his kid brother. Anyway, Dave works for the firm that's been hired to analyze all the data and make a report. Dave called this morning and told me, off the record, that at this point everyone from the engineer to the architect is pointing fingers at someone else. But . . .''

Kara didn't have to hear it to know that most fingers were being pointed at their father. She asked Hank to stay in touch with Dave and let her know if he heard anything more. In the meantime, she'd soon draw her first paycheck and would send them every penny she could.

"Believe me, it'll help. You're a good sister and daughter. The best."

"I'm trying. I don't know what else to do. Any updates on when you'll be able to go back to work?"

Hank sighed. "A couple of months, or so they keep telling me. The physical therapist suggested I look into computer training since it's a lot safer. Can you see me sitting inside all day looking at some blinking little screen?"

No. She couldn't, just as she couldn't see letting her father go through this nightmare alone. As soon as the timing felt right, she'd tell him that either he stop trying to protect her and Hank or she'd go to Brand; she couldn't play it any other way.

When Hank asked how things were going between her and her boss, she told him that they'd gone toe to toe over something that had happened earlier in the week. Since then they'd both been so busy that they'd barely had time to say two words to each other. "You know how it is. Tempers flare sometimes, then things cool down."

"I hope so. You've got enough on your mind without being at odds with the man. What's he like?"

"To work for? Competent. He's a hands-on boss."

"So I've heard. Sis? I don't remember much of what happened the day of the accident, but I have a picture of Lockwood in my mind. You're not going to let yourself get distracted by what he looks like, are you?"

For a few seconds she didn't answer. Then: "That's not what I'm here for."

"I know that. But sometimes—that's the last thing any

of us need—look, forget I said anything. Just take care of yourself, okay?''

"I will. And you do the same."

"Friday night! Look out world, I'm going to howl!''
Kara laughed at the expression on the Indian woman's face. "In Skagway?" she asked. "I haven't seen any place where a person could howl."

"That shows what you know. There's a bar behind the Prospector's Lodge that caters to locals who've been punching a time clock too long. I discovered it my second night here. Cheap, cold beer and eardrum-busting live country and western music. What more could you want out of life?''

Beer, to Kara's way of thinking, was highly overrated, but the way Stella put it made an hour or so in a bar sound exactly like what she needed. The nights puttering around alone in her cabin, worrying about her father, trying to decide what and when she'd say something to Brand had made her more than a little frayed around the edges. When Stella suggested she join the others for some serious kicking back, she agreed.

After work she followed Stella down the mountain, through town, and behind the Prospector's Lodge. The parking lots at the front and sides of the lodge were clogged with dusty tour buses, but tucked away on a graveled alley stood a less than straight weathered and unpainted building with a bright purple door. The coats of paint didn't quite cover the door's battered condition. *Gold Dust Bar* the sign read. *Liv music Fr., Sat. nights.*

"See," Stella announced the moment they stepped inside. "What did I tell you? Kickin' back time."

At first all Kara could see was a smoke-blue haze, vague outlines of people—lots of people—but after a few minutes her eyes became accustomed to the gloom, and she dared step away from the door. One side of the loud,

packed interior was crammed with tiny tables and uncom-
fortable-looking chairs. A bar already filled with mugs in
various stages of use took up the far wall. To the left was
a raised stage where three young musicians were warming
up. The dance floor looked as if it might hold a half dozen
couples, as long as none of them took up much space.

For a moment, Kara's attention was drawn to a flashing
neon sign hung over one of the two windows in the place.
Only half of the sign was lit up, casting the faces of weary
men and women in reddish hues. "It's interesting," she
observed tongue in cheek.

"Interesting? Woman, you need a drink."

Kara didn't argue with Stella. And even if she'd tried,
it would have been a lost cause since Stella was already
weaving her way around the tables, her attention riveted
on the bartender.

Kara followed as close behind as she could, stopping
briefly twice to acknowledge those who called out to her
in rowdy greeting. From what she could tell, half of those
here were on Brand's crew. The rest looked like locals—
faded work shirts and blue jeans instead of the bright poly-
ester so many of the tourists wore. She could feel the long
hours of physical labor seep out of her, inch by inch,
second by second. These people made up the only world
she'd ever known; she wanted and needed to be with them.

When Stella handed her a frosty mug, Kara lifted it to
her lips and swallowed. Not bad. Before she could take a
second sip, Stella grabbed her arm and steered her toward
a table where two native women already sat hunched over
a bowl of pretzels. Kara plunked herself down and gave
the other women the thumbs up sign. The band—guitar,
drums, banjo—began belting out a song about a long haul
trucker and some woman who was waiting for him, not
with wine and dinner, but a shotgun.

She loved it!

"Just you wait." Stella placed her mouth near Kara's

ear and yelled. "Give these jokers a couple more beers and you'll have to beat them off with a stick."

Stella was right about that. She'd just finished the beer Stella had bought her when Chuck wandered over with another, which he insisted she drink because she looked thirsty enough to dry up and blow away. He introduced her to the woman with him but she didn't catch the name, just that Chuck obviously was delighted with this particular company.

Kara sipped at the foam, but before she could pick up the mug, someone tapped her on the shoulder. Sid something. Sid had an itch to dance and wasn't about to take no for an answer. Although Stella shook her head no, Kara joined him on the dance floor. Within a few seconds she understood Stella's warning. Sid might make a great grape stomper, but he couldn't dance. Sid was replaced by a bearded beanpole named Raymond Smith or Jones or Johnson who danced as if he'd taken lessons from Sid. After that she lost count; she barely had time to finish the beer Chuck had brought her.

No one tried to put a serious make on her. Instead, all they seemed interested in was unwinding a bit. Good. That's what she wanted. Because the band apparently didn't know any slow songs, she didn't have to worry about being crushed in the arms of some overenthusiastic partner. Instead, she could concentrate on the inroads the loud, deep, pounding sounds made on her senses.

There was something about country and western, something strong and basic and honest. Shotguns and old pickup trucks instead of structural diagnosticians and courts. She'd have to tell Hank that. If only he could see her now—he and their father.

The song had ended. After thanking her partner, a short, solid man with enough of a beard to make a grizzly proud, she started toward her table. Her feet ached and she wished she'd taken time to change out of her boots. Maybe a pretzel would revive her.

"Kara?"

Was it possible for a single whisper to override every other sound? Before she had time to search for the answer to her question, she felt Brand's hand on her shoulder and no longer cared. He'd removed his hard hat. The wind had dried his hair, lifted and filled it until she wondered if she could lose her fingers in it. His jeans embraced his hips, increased her awareness of him.

"Would you like to dance?"

She hadn't seen him come in, had told herself she didn't care whether he showed.

But she did. Caution, wisdom aside, she needed this time with him. "Yes. I'd like that."

He swung her around so that she faced him. Feeling somehow sheltered by him, she waited for the next song to begin. "I could hear the music before I got out of my truck," he said. "When I looked at the building, I swore it was vibrating."

She couldn't hear everything he said, but by concentrating on his lips, she made out enough that she could nod agreement. He said something else. That she didn't catch.

"What?"

He leaned closer, bent down. "I said, they need to expand."

It was a simple comment. Why then did she feel a shiver chase down her spine simply because his breath touched her ear? She wasn't sure what, if anything, she should say in response, but before she had more than a couple of seconds in which to think about that, someone called out Brand's name. He turned toward the other man, his arm around her shoulder so they wouldn't be separated. She caught snatches of what the two were saying—something about a transmission. Then the drummer drove his stick against a cymbal and began a furious tattoo of sound that enveloped her senses.

She felt herself being pulled into Brand's arms, then released so they could each dance as the music directed them, felt the hard driving tempo fill her. Not caring what she was doing, she moved with the music, arms and legs and body racing to keep up with the sound. She felt free, wild. On the brink of danger. A few inches away Brand matched her beat for beat. She saw his hair lift and fall, his face flush, his muscular body work in perfect sync with the drumbeat. It wasn't a dance for touching. Occasionally their arms brushed, but that was all.

Or was it? Even with hot, electric space between them, his presence was all but overwhelming. She wanted to drown in him, needed to press her body against his.

To know what it felt like to be a woman in the arms of a sexy, sexy man.

Was he teasing her? Surely he couldn't be unaware of his impact on her. But although his eyes remained fixed on hers and his body continued to call to hers, she couldn't climb into his mind and know what lived there.

Maybe the wanting was only in her.

Finally, the song ended. She ached with the loss; she needed to regain her sense of self. "Do you want to try it again?" he asked as the drummer teased his drums.

Yes. Oh, God, yes! "No. I—" She took a deep breath of overheated air. "I need to catch my breath."

"Not in here."

She couldn't argue that. The air felt so close that it was impossible to draw a decent breath. He didn't say anything else, only took her arm and led her through the mass of people and out the purple door. She felt his heat, his strength. Air. Maybe cold Alaska air would help.

Because the summer sun was still high in the sky, she couldn't tell how long she'd been in the bar. She was a little lightheaded from having two beers on an empty stomach, unable to control her reaction to her boss. "My ears are still ringing," she told him because she wouldn't tell him the rest of what she felt. "And something tells me I'm going to have a headache."

"I take it you don't do that kind of thing very often."

"No. I don't." She lifted her shirt away from her throat and made a fanning motion to cool herself. Brand had leaned against the side of the building. He watched her.

"I—" *Get a grip*, she chided herself. She'd been watched by men before. But the beers, the heat—Brand's heat . . . "I don't often join in something like this, the Friday night letting go."

"When you were married, you had other things to do."

"I wasn't married very long, Brand. I—" She almost told him that a large part of the reason she didn't join the drinking crowd was that she'd always been the boss's daughter. "I guess it's just not my style, at least not most of the time."

Brand had started frowning before she finished speaking. He still looked puzzled. "You weren't married very long?"

"Less than a year."

"Do you ever see him?"

Why did Brand care about that? She explained that she hadn't seen Scott for a year and a half now. From what she'd heard, he was engaged to a college student. "I wish him the best."

"Do you?"

"Oh, yes." She ran the back of her hand over her forehead. The music still shook the air, but it had become muted now, a backdrop for conversation. "I've never understood people who hold grudges. Certainly—" She grinned. "I'd never take off after Scott with a shotgun."

"A shotgun?"

She explained about the first song she'd heard that

night. "I believe in letting people live their own lives. As long as they do the same with me, I'm happy."

"Unfortunately, life isn't always like that."

She didn't want to discuss anything serious tonight, not with the air smelling of Alaska and Brand Lockwood standing beside her. But if it was up to her to keep the conversation going, she wasn't sure she'd be able to contribute a thing. She leaned against the wall and let it support her head, feeling the building vibrate against her shoulder. Vibrate through her.

Because she'd turned so that she could look at Brand, she knew he hadn't taken his eyes off her. "No, it isn't," she finally came up with. "Sometimes there's someone with a shotgun waiting for you."

"I've never had that happen. The truth is, I've never wanted it."

"See what you've missed. If you had, maybe you would have written a song about it and gotten rich."

He hit his temple with the back of his hand, looking crushed. "Song writing. Do you know anything about it?"

"Not a thing. It's probably too late for either of us to start. Oh well, I didn't want to go through life with a headache from the sound anyway."

"I didn't think about that. And since I don't know a musical note from the proverbial hole in the ground, I'd better stick with my day job. Speaking of jobs, about earlier this week—" As a trio of brightly dressed middle-aged women walked around the corner of the motel, Brand stopped talking. The women stared at them, at the bar, then turned and hurried away. Brand grinned, but after a moment turned serious again. "Thank you. For not bailing out. If I'd lost the equipment, I might be out of work."

She'd known that but hadn't been going to mention it. By way of answer, she simply shrugged.

"I'll say it again. Thank you—even if, no, just thank you."

"You're welcome."

"I like the way you reacted when I jumped on you. You gave me back just what I dished out."

"I did that, didn't I?" She gave him a wry smile. "And you weren't the only one who jumped. We were both acting on nerves."

"True."

"I talked to Montana," Kara said. "He promised not to dump any more gravel that close to the edge."

"I know. I approached him about the same thing. He said you'd already gotten the point across. Said you talk more like a foreman than a 'dozer operator."

Kara nodded but said nothing. Did she want the conversation to go on in this direction? If she hadn't had those two beers, she might be able to concentrate more fully, to zero in on the tone of Brand's voice, the look in his eyes, her reactions to him.

As she stood there trying to collect her thoughts, the three tourists again peeked around the corner of the building. This time Brand gave them his full attention. "No one in there is going to bite, ladies," he said. "They're loud but safe."

"We just wanted to get a little local color," one of the women explained. "Do you think they'd mind if we took pictures?"

Brand winced, then winked at Kara. "I'm not sure that's such a hot idea. You'd have to use flash and that's pretty disruptive. Those are hard working folks in there, not props provided by the chamber of commerce. What if you step in for a few minutes, listen and watch. Maybe someone will ask you to dance."

The three began talking and giggling among themselves. One obviously wanted to take Brand up on his suggestion. The other two weren't sure that was a good idea. Although the women made her want to laugh, Kara was disappointed that the conversation between her and Brand had been interrupted. A few more minutes and she might have had a better reading on what made the man tick.

Or would she? This was Friday night, time to kick back and relax. Between her reaction to Brand and the beers her mind had all it could hold onto.

She pushed away from the wall and took a step toward her pickup. Did she really want to go home? Tell him goodnight? "I don't think I'm up to going back in there," she admitted. "My head and ears are putting up a powerful protest."

"Me either. Let's walk. My roommate's going to be using our place pretty soon. He suggested I give him a little space."

Ten minutes later they stood looking out at the gray quiet of the Lynn Canal. The wind blew freely here, and although it wasn't all that cold, Kara felt better moving than she did standing still. She'd said something about finding it hard to believe that the residents of Skagway didn't seem bothered by being so dependent for transportation on hundreds of miles of inland waterway.

By way of answer, Brand pointed at the massive, gleaming cruise ship docked at the weathered dock. "The ship seems such a contrast, the ultimate in luxury next to something that has to survive everything nature can and does throw at it." He wrapped his arm around her shoulder, a gentle gesture. She could have pulled free; she should have. But, despite everything, she'd wanted to feel his hand on her from that first day in his trailer. Tonight, for a few minutes, she would let it happen.

"I don't know about cruises," she said softly. Something had made her feel philosophical; she went with the mood. "I guess they're all right, but I'm not much for herd activities. If I ever explore Alaska, really explore it, I'm going to throw a camper on my truck and go where I want, when I want."

"You wouldn't do it with a sled and team of dogs?"

"No, thank you. I'll leave that to hardier souls." She couldn't take her eyes off the seemingly endless stretch of water that had brought the massive ship here. Had the tourists looked out at their surroundings as they made their way to Skagway and been overwhelmed by the sense of space? With the mountains rising in all directions, making a lie of everything she thought she knew about space and distance, she didn't see how it could be otherwise. No matter how many people the ship carried, what its horse-power was, or how well it was built, next to the wilderness, it was nothing.

Tonight she felt like nothing.

As if reading her mind, Brand pointed toward the mountain they'd go back to trying to tame tomorrow. "Looking at that, I feel like a fraud."

"A fraud?"

He ran his hand down her arm a few inches, warming flesh, making her feel as if they were the only two people in the world. "For being so presumptuous as to think I can alter this awesome vastness in any way. Maybe— maybe we ought to just leave Alaska the way it is."

Was Brand aware of how much he was revealing to her? From having grown up around construction workers, she knew how fiercely they worked to maintain their macho images. Not many would admit to qualms about what they were doing. Even fewer would show a philo-sophical side. "No one's ever going to tame the mountains of Alaska. Mother Nature will make sure of that. All you'll do is touch it a little."

"I hope you're right."

She glanced up at him. He looked as serious as he always did, and yet his eyes seemed to have softened a little. Maybe because she gave him something other than work and commitment to think about.

Maybe because he was aware that they'd isolated them-selves from the rest of the world.

"I hope I am, too," she whispered. "Man has altered enough of this world for his own purpose. They have to leave these mountains alone."

"I want to come back in a thousand years and find things exactly the way they are tonight."

Her attention was drawn to a sea gull flying over the cruise ship. It dipped low as if checking something on the deck, then swooped up again. Its flight took it in front of the wildly flapping flags. Behind the flags stood snow-sheltered granite peaks that had always, almost always, been in existence.

Without thinking about what she was doing, Kara laid her head against Brand's shoulder. She pointed at the sea gull. "He's so free," she whispered. "Nothing controls him except the wind."

"That and his appetite."

"True," she acknowledged, unwilling to let go of her pensive mood—or the warm presence beside her. "I've always wanted to strap myself into a glider. To let the wind take me where it wants."

"What if the wind deserted you?"

"Then I guess I'd fall." She had her feet planted firmly on the ground. She wasn't at all worried about a glider accident.

"No, you wouldn't."

"I wouldn't? Why not?"

"Because I wouldn't let you."

She gave a half thought to asking how he could keep a promise like that, but when she looked up at him, she lost herself in his eyes. In the message in them. In her primi-tive answer.

I want to kiss you, his eyes said.

Yes, her heart answered. *Yes.*

FIVE

Brand followed Kara back to her place. When he got out of his truck, a half-interested, tongue-dragging large black dog emerged from somewhere and sniffed at his boot. Kara had absolutely no need to be escorted home, but he didn't want the evening to end yet, and she hadn't objected.

After a minute the dog leaned against his leg and stared up at him as if to let him know he wasn't used to being kept up so late. "I know how you feel," he said as he leaned over to pat him on the head. "These long days take a lot out of a fellow, don't they? What you need is a nap."

As if Brand's suggestion had given the Lab permission to stop playing watchdog, he flopped onto his belly. Two seconds later he'd rested his head on his front legs.

The dog no longer held Brand's attention.

Kara stood with her fingers still wrapped around her truck door handle, waiting for him, hitting him again with the potent femininity that simmered beneath jeans and flannel shirt.

It hadn't been much of a kiss, quick, gentle, on the

brink, a peck. But what coursed through him at that moment hadn't been at all like a reaction to a peck. He'd been grateful to the cool, vibrant sea breeze for the way it slapped at him as they pulled away from each other and continued walking, jolting him back to reality. Otherwise—otherwise he might have given in to need and want. Might have believed the message he told himself he saw in her eyes.

Did she regret it? Was she even now wondering what her boss meant by coming onto her? "Coming on." The words sounded crude, nothing like what he'd intended. What he'd experienced. What he wanted.

When she continued to watch him, the evergreens serving as her backdrop, it took him a good fifteen seconds to come up with something to say, a way of drawing out the leavetaking. "I was just thinking." His voice sounded too deep. He swallowed and tried again. "Despite what I just told our friend here, it's a good thing it stays light as long as it does this time of year. Otherwise, with all these trees and no street lights, it'd be hard finding your way in the dark. You might wind up falling over what's his name."

"Mooch. Oh, I think I'd manage. I have a good sense when it comes to moving about at night."

"Being in the dark doesn't bother you?"

She laughed, went on looking at him. "Hardly. I've worked at too many remote places to let that kind of thing get to me."

He shouldn't have asked the stupid question. Of course, she wouldn't be spooked by the night. What, if anything, was she afraid of? It was none of his business, and he didn't want to be drawn into a discussion that might lead him to telling her he still had nightmares about buildings collapsing around him. He avoided it by simply walking ahead of her as they crossed the rickety old bridge. With every passing second, he expected her to tell him it was time for him to go home, but she didn't.

Did she want him around? Maybe. He wished he could be surer about that, but there was a tenseness about her he couldn't dismiss. It had faded for a few minutes while they danced and again when their eyes met in silent message and they played at a kiss, but now he felt the tension swirling around her again, just as the breeze tossed its way through tree branches.

Why?

Had her ex done some kind of a number on her? Maybe it was him. Maybe she didn't want a personal relationship with her boss. Only, it was already too late for that, and she'd have to be a fool not to know that.

"There." Her word came out in a soft sigh. "There it is, in all its glory."

He glanced at the cabin now only a few feet away. Then he took another look. "It really is a one-man job, isn't it? That's quite a roof. They didn't go overboard securing it, did they?" He cocked his head, pretending to give it his expert scrutiny. "Makes you wonder whether the place would pass any building codes."

"That's important to you? Even cabins have to conform to official standards?"

Something about her tone set him on edge. Wondering at her words, he explained that as far as the cabin was concerned, the only thing he cared was that it didn't fall down around its occupant. He admired whoever had built it, armed, it appeared, with nothing more than a saw and hammer. "A lot of what we do in this world is over-regulated. Believe me, I've seen enough of that. What concerns me is safety."

She went on looking at the cabin's indistinct outline. "Just as long as you don't let your zeal get in the way of common sense."

"Zeal? Common sense? Kara, I was joking about this place passing building codes. I don't know why—"

"Were you? The way you go on about safety, you'd think—"

"Yeah, I do go on about it. And I'm not going to change." He turned on her. No matter what her reaction, he had to tell her this. "I broke my back because someone ignored safety standards. For almost two weeks I didn't know whether I would ever walk again."

Even surrounded by deep shadows, he could see— sense—her turn pale. "I–I didn't know."

"I know you didn't," he said, careful to keep his tone gentle. "But lying flat on my back at nineteen, not sure whether I'd ever get out of that bed on my own power, made a lifelong impact."

She stepped closer, reached out and touched his cheek with less than steady fingers. For too long she said nothing. He read in her eyes a lifetime of emotion, but couldn't tap what was going through her. Finally: "I'm sorry."

"Don't be," he said around his stirring senses. "I healed. I even make a stab at dancing."

She didn't laugh. For a moment he thought she might tell him what she was thinking, hoped she would. Instead, she let her hand drop back by her side and looked around at her surroundings. She seemed to retreat into herself, take up less space. "I wish I'd known."

"Known what?" He didn't want to talk about that time in his life any more.

After another moment of silence, he sensed her pulling herself out of wherever it was she'd gone. Still when she smiled, he could tell she'd had to work at making it happen. "I was thinking, we tell ourselves we know someone, and then we learn something new, and it puts a whole different perspective on things. Makes everything more complicated."

"Complicated?"

"Yes. I, ah, I don't mean to keep you."

"You aren't." For three, maybe four seconds he debated the wisdom of touching her. Then, ignoring the possibility that she might bolt if he did, he took her hand and eased her a few inches closer to him. She met his gaze. He read both tension and caution. Still, she allowed the contact to continue. "Thanks," she said softly. "For dancing with me. And getting me out of there before I passed out from a lack of oxygen." She blinked. "And for the walk."

"I'm the one who should be thanking you, Kara. After the way I jumped at you earlier this week, I wouldn't have been surprised if you'd told me to take a hike."

"I can't do that."

Can't do that? What was she talking about? When he felt her trying to draw free, he held on and searched his mind for a way to keep things going between them. What he came up with surprised him. "I've been thinking about something. Ada and Cliff suggested we explore Skagway and the land around it. Would you like to do that? It might give us a better perspective of history." *Did he give a damn about history?*

"I—all right."

All right. He'd seen more enthusiasm over a dentist appointment. "When?"

"Whenever." Again she tried to free herself. "You must have other things to do. I mean, you have so little free time."

None as important as trying to figure you out. "Kara? What is it?"

She opened her mouth. Still, it seemed to take her a long, long time to speak. "You're my boss. Our relationship . . ."

"What about it? Are you worried what others might think?"

"No," she said quickly and he believed her. "That's

our business, not theirs. But we're employer and employee. What if I do something you can't live with? If you have to fire me—''

''Will you give that a rest. I'm not going to fire you.''

She'd been looking at his chest. Now she lifted her head and met his eyes. ''You don't know that.''

What was her preoccupation with job security? Surely she knew that with her job skills, she could get on with any crew. ''If you're telling me I can't look into the future, you're right,'' he acknowledged. ''But I've spent a week now watching you work. You're a pro, and I don't shoot myself in the foot by firing pros.''

That elicited the faintest smile from her. ''I can't see you ever shooting yourself in the foot. You don't do anything impulsive.''

Asking her to dance, taking her down to the canal, walking her home, wanting to kiss her wasn't impulsive? Still, he didn't tell her that. Instead he gave in to what had to be the most impulsive act of the evening. She'd stopped trying to pull free; now she stood waiting—waiting for him?

He turned thought into action.

For a fleeting second he wished she was wearing what she'd been the other evening after her shower, but even in her workday clothes he was aware—damned aware—of the woman beneath the layers of fabric. When he eased her against him, she tensed, shuddered, didn't quite mold herself into him.

He slid his hands over her back and brought her closer. Again he sensed the battle in her and waited her out. He should release her; a gentleman would do exactly that. But tonight, what he felt had nothing to do with gentlemanly conduct.

He wanted to challenge her with the only weapon he had—himself.

Then she surrendered to his silent dare and he felt her

lips touch his and the questions running through him were silenced. Someday, somehow, he'd get her to tell him what was behind her emotional wars and his role in them. But not now.

He'd been without a woman to care about for too long.

Care? The word shot through him, but with Kara's essence filling him, he couldn't hold onto it. He didn't remember pressing his fingertips into the small of her back and pulling her tight against him, but he must have. She felt so slight and vulnerable and defenseless under the thick flannel. The knowledge teased and tested him.

He didn't try to wrench free of the test. Instead he deepened their kiss, forcing her to part her lips. He could hear her breathe; he could hear himself try to draw in enough air to keep his head clear.

What did it matter? It was Friday night, so late that even the summer Alaskan sun was fading. She was here, in his arms, giving him a precious piece of herself. And he wanted her—primitive and unthinking. Inch by inch he worked his hands upward until he buried one in the hair at the base of her neck. Sliding his fingers around the satiny strands, he drew her head back, increasing his power over her. His body responded, hot and male. He sucked in night air. His mind remained knotted around thoughts, impressions of her.

He could take her, now, here. If that's what she wanted. She didn't.

When he felt her stiffen again and try to wrench her head free, he ordered himself to stop feeling and begin thinking. She shook her head from side to side, her breath now ragged and quick. "Kara?" Brand released her, drew back a step. "What is it?"

"I don't—I'm not ready for this."

Why? "Tell me something, please. Are you still hung up about my being your boss? I told you—"

"I know what you said. But . . ."

He waited, kept on waiting for her to say more, but silence stretched out between them until he gave up trying to reach her. Reluctantly he let his hands drop by his side and looked down at her, aware of her large, dark eyes on him, the mane of hair that had half freed itself from whatever she'd tried to contain it with. He read caution, distrust, and a simple longing for something she'd never had. At least he told himself that's what he saw. "I have to go," she whispered.

"For tonight," he whispered back. "But sometime . . ."

"Sometime what?"

"You're going to tell me what's going on inside you. He turned you inside out. That's not right."

"He?"

"Your ex-husband. Someone."

Kara didn't sleep well, but then she hadn't expected to. Finally, she got up a half hour before her alarm was set to go off and, after a cup of coffee, washed out a few pieces of underwear in the undersized kitchen sink. Laundry didn't give her enough to put her mind to.

Last night kept intruding.

Each time she tried to focus on what Brand had said about Scott being behind the way she'd reacted, her thoughts slid away to the time she and Brand had spent dancing and then walking along the dock.

Her life was firmly planted in reality, machinery, quick decisions. It had always been like that. Watching sea gulls and talking about hang gliding, surrendering to the energy in her, had nothing to do with reason. He wanted to explore Skagway with her, and even though that was the last thing she should ever do with Brand Lockwood, it was exactly what she wanted. Maybe, she told herself, if they shared that experience, telling him who she was wouldn't be as hard. Their relationship would have deepened. The tie would be stronger. And more dangerous?

Yes.

But that would happen later. For now, she had to clear up certain misconceptions.

That opportunity came during Saturday's lunch break. She'd noticed that a fair number of the crew acted as if they'd overindulged last night and were popping aspirin trying to get over their hangovers. However, by noon most had regained their appetites and energy. She sat near the Indian women she'd been with in the bar, wondering whether they'd say anything about her having left with the boss. Stella did. "Not that I blame you." She winked. "If I wasn't happily married to the second biggest trucker in Alaska, I'd have set my sights on Lockwood myself. He's a gentleman, is he?"

"Yes." Kara concentrated on her sandwich.

"Well, that's no fun. Any chance you can change his mind?"

"I'm not interested in changing his mind. Right now that kind of relationship is the last thing I need."

Stella laughed. "How many times have I heard that? Said it enough times myself before Butch came along. Speaking of bosses, here he comes."

Brand straddled a deep rut and easily hoisted his body over it. He nodded at Stella. "I wanted to tell you, that wasn't a wolf you thought you saw in the trees yesterday. I threw out some meat this morning and this huge, gray dog made short work of it. He's so wild I couldn't get within twenty feet of him. He also looks well fed."

"A dog." Stella snorted the word. "A wolf would have been a lot more interesting. Made for a better story. So, how's it going? Anyone too hungover to work?"

"Close. Close." Brand inclined his head at Kara, acknowledging her presence for the first time. "I hate to tell you, but I think your tailpipe's on its last legs."

"I know it's on its last legs." Kara shook her head and sighed. "I've got to weld a new bracket to the frame to hold it in place. Otherwise, I'm going to leave it on the road somewhere."

"Why are you trying to salvage it? It's so corroded a stiff wind's going to blow it away."

"Tell me about it. But where am I going to find a replacement up here? I thought maybe I could coax a few more miles out of it."

"That's what I was going to tell you. Chuck's got a spare tailpipe in the bed of his truck. Don't ask me where he got it. He's a packrat. If it fits, I'm sure he'll let you have it."

When Brand pointed toward Chuck's rig, she got to her feet and followed Brand over to it. Once she glanced back over her shoulder. Stella was shaking her finger at her and laughing.

The tailpipe would work. After telling Brand that, she searched her mind for a way to bring up what she needed to say. In the end, she came right out with it. "I think you got the wrong impression last night. From what you said, it sounds as if you think I had a traumatic marriage and divorce. The experience wasn't something I'd ever want to repeat, but I've hardly been scarred by it."

"Oh."

He wasn't making this easy for her. Or maybe the problem was that she couldn't forget those moments in his arms and her unsuccessful battle to pretend they hadn't happened—or that she'd wanted them to happen. "Scott's a gentle man, a precise, intelligent, orderly man who needs a woman like him. I wasn't that woman."

"Oh."

"He's traditional, at least the stereotype of the traditional man. Scott needs a stereotypical wife, not one who drives a bulldozer for a living."

"I see."

"We tried, at least I thought we did. When I fell in love with him, I told myself our love would transcend any

differences." *Shut up. Why'd you ever get started on this?*
"My family tried to tell me I was being naive and Scott
and I were too different, but—well, you know how young
love is."

"What young love isn't is smart. Believe me, I speak
from experience."

She could laugh at that. "No. It isn't. Mostly it gets
bruised and has its feelings hurt."

"You'll get no arguments from me."

"Hopefully I learned from my experience. Scott and I
bruised each other a lot." *Why was she rattling on?* "I
tried to fit myself into the round hole but I was still a
square peg. Finally—" She sighed. "Finally I got tired
of trying. End of story."

"Is it?" He was staring at her with his head slightly
cocked to one side. His shave had been a once over
lightly; he looked rugged, too rugged.

"What do you mean?"

He rammed his hands in his back pockets, a gesture
she'd already learned was an integral part of him. It wasn't
fair; a man, this man, shouldn't have shoulders that wide.
"Something's got you turned inside out."

Am I that transparent? "That's what you think?"

"That's what I think. You're like that wild dog, shying
away when I get too close."

She almost told him she didn't appreciate being com-
pared to something with four legs, but he'd nearly touched
on the truth so she didn't. Instead, because nothing had
changed and she still believed she needed to forge a relationship with him, she concentrated on his rough honesty.
Gave back in kind. "If I'm shying, it's because I didn't
expect to wind up dancing with my boss and talking
about—personal things."

His eyes, his body even seemed to gentle a little. "It
isn't a crime."

Of course it wasn't, but he had no idea how complicated

things were for her. "Brand, I respect you. You're good, very good at what you do. I'm used to respecting the people I work for." *My father most of all.* "But when that gets tangled up with other things . . ."

"What kind of other things?"

"You must know the answer to that. What we shared last night—don't make me spell it out."

"I won't. I don't have to." He pulled his hands out of his pockets and let them hang by his side. The gesture reminded her that she hadn't seen him limp today and hadn't noticed any weakness in his leg while they were dancing and walking last night. If that meant he'd been able to put the physical aspect of the accident behind him, maybe—maybe she could test what else about the accident he might now have in a different, less vengeful perspective. But not today with hours of work still ahead of them and who knew how many eyes on them. Not while she so feared his answers.

"I really haven't dated anyone seriously since my divorce," she said even though she didn't owe him an explanation. "I spent six months working on the coast, another three on a bridge project in southern Oregon last fall—well, you know how it is. When you know you aren't going to be in one place very long, you keep wondering if its worth the effort."

"Yeah. I know. Moving with the job ended things for me and someone I cared for, more than once."

She nodded. "And with you . . ." What had she gotten herself into? She was talking as if he'd asked her to go to bed with him when all they'd shared was a kiss. So far. "You're my boss."

"You said that before." He sucked in a deep breath and slowly let it out. "This is getting complicated, isn't it?"

"Very."

"More complicated than it needs to be."

No, Brand. You're wrong.

When the crew went back to work, Brand cornered Chuck long enough to tell him that Kara was interested in his tailpipe. Then, even though there were a thousand things he could be doing, he wandered back to where he'd seen the meat-mooching dog earlier. Although he whistled several times, the dog didn't put in an appearance.

What was going on with him? It wasn't as if Kara Richardson was his first female employee. Granted, a lot of them had signed on with their husbands. The unattached ones had seldom appealed to him for a variety of reasons. Either they were much older than he or so singleminded about their determination to prove themselves in a predominantly male world that he'd found it easier all the way around to keep the relationship professional.

It was different with Kara Richardson, and he didn't know why.

All right, he had a hint, more than a hint, he thought as he headed for his truck. He'd have to be dead and buried not to be physically aware of her. She cared for Cliff and Ada and he liked that. She did her job, damn well. She was intelligent and curious, both gentle and strong. Beautiful and physically self-confident about herself.

She also, no matter how much she tried to explain it away, was almost as shy as that wild dog around him.

So? So what?

So, he didn't want it like that between them.

Why?

Because she's an attractive, bright, desirable woman, he answered his own question. And after what he'd been through recently and still wasn't done with, he needed to be reminded that there was more to life than seeing that justice was done.

Barely aware of what he was doing, he climbed into the cab, started the engine, and, hugging the graveled side, eased around the endless line of vehicles. Most of the drivers gave him a long, envious look. A few glared.

Maybe what he needed to do was tell her that. Straight out let her know that he wanted to balance out his life, and if she was willing to be part of that, they'd make it work. He'd hand her honesty about himself and ask her to do the same. She'd tell him what was going on inside her head, and he'd understand and they'd go on from there.

And maybe he should forget the whole thing.

SIX

"Oh, my goodness, they're already here."

Kara hurried over to where Ada was looking out the front window. Although it was barely eight o'clock on Sunday morning and she'd just offered to make coffee for Cliff and Ada, the crew was arriving. Obviously they'd all parked out by the bridge, but they'd hiked in to satisfy their curiosity about what was at the end of the narrow road. Kara counted eight, Brand leading the way. "I'm impressed," she told Ada. She fingered her shirt button, glad she'd showered and dressed as soon as she got up. "Either they're unbelievably conscientious or Brand is really cracking the whip."

Ada continued to stare. Kara moved aside so Cliff could join them. "I had no idea there'd be so many," Ada said. "They'll never fit in the house."

Kara headed for the front door, explaining over her shoulder that the men and women hadn't come to drink coffee and visit. Still, she understood Ada's agitation. When Brand called last night to explain that the crew would be there bright and early the next morning, Ada had gone into a tizzy trying to pick up the cluttered living room. It had taken a while but Kara, who'd been there visiting and once again trying to get through to her father, had been able to settle Ada down so they could concentrate on what needed to be done. Now, however, it looked as if she'd have her hands full today keeping Ada and Cliff out of the way.

When she stepped outside, Chuck bowed elaborately, then shot a stream of tobacco juice toward the bushes. He indicated the still bleary-eyed crew, most of whom were looking over at the cabin. "Your servants have arrived, milady. All we ask is a little kindness. And maybe a few scraps of food and a sip of brew when we're done." He held up the thermos that had been dangling from his fingers. "We all brought our own jolts of coffee."

Smiling, Kara informed him that a barbecue, complete with something cold to drink, was being planned. All they had to provide was their appetites.

"You done good," Chuck informed her. "A certain friend of mine might show up a little later. You wouldn't mind if she had a bite, too, would you?"

"Of course not." Kara glanced around. "She isn't here now?"

Chuck looked sheepish. At least he tried to. "I kept her up a little late last night. Since my roommate—" He indicated Brand. "Since he wasn't too crazy about sleeping out in his truck, I had to scrounge up a motel room."

Brand shook his head. "My heart bleeds for you."

"Why don't I believe you? Oh well, it was a—how should I say this—an entertaining evening."

Groaning, Brand winked at Kara. "So he's said, twice already."

As the crew started wandering back to the bridge, Kara joined Chuck and a freshly shaven Brand in the front yard. She laughed as Ada and Cliff went off with the men. "I'll do my best to keep them out of your hair," she told Brand. "But they're so excited."

Brand watched Cliff and Ada for a moment, his mouth quirked in amusement. "I can see that. I don't want to run roughshod over them, so if they've said anything about how they want the work done, I'd appreciate it if you'd clue me in."

Kara explained that Cliff had been trying to work up a sketch, a blueprint he called it, but every time he showed it to Ada, she found something wrong with it. She suggested Brand confer with Cliff and Ada separately, thank them for their input, and then do what needed to be done.

It was a rare Alaska morning. Not a cloud was in the sky and although that might change at any moment, she was determined to enjoy it to the utmost. In Brand's presence.

Chuck left to head for the bridge. He said he wanted to supervise the tearing up of the old bridge to see if the timbers could be used as firewood. His long legs made it possible for him to quickly catch up with Cliff and Ada, and Kara watched the trio until they were out of sight.

"I love those two," she told Brand. "Cliff reminds me so much of my father."

"Does he? In what way?"

Although she might be coming close to a landmine, Kara took advantage of the opportunity to paint Art Crayton as she knew and loved him, without revealing who he was. That way Brand would have a picture of the private man. "My dad's so stubborn that he makes a mule look like a pushover," she admitted. "The more I point out how bullheaded he is, the more he digs in. Sometimes I think he does it just to get me riled."

"It sounds as if he succeeds."

She chuckled, breathed deeply. Brand had used aftershave, a senses-filling scent that reminded her of a sun-baked forest. "Not really," she managed despite the unexpected, tantalizing distraction. "It's just his way of keeping me on my toes. He believes that a man—or a woman—has to stand on his or her own two feet. He has absolutely nothing in common with the corporate animal and no desire to change things.''

Brand turned as if to follow the others. When she didn't move, he touched her shoulder, indicating he wanted her to join him. The day became even brighter simply because she felt his warmth. Because she couldn't ignore the impact of his aftershave.

After a few seconds of pure emotion, she thought to fall in line with him. ''The world needs more people like my father. Someone who takes responsibility for his actions—'' Should she say this? Or would Brand one day call her a liar? ''Who has the courage of his convictions.''

''As long as he doesn't do that with his head stuck in the sand.''

Had he guessed? No. How could he? ''That's true,'' she admitted, weighing her every word. ''What you're saying is, the world is continually changing and that old warhorses like my father have to keep up with the times.''

''Something like that.''

Wondering if Brand had grown tired of the subject, she glanced over at him. He was looking at the horizon, a slightly wistful expression sliding over his strong features. ''Look at that. The sky goes on forever. I don't know how else to describe it. I was just thinking,'' he said slowly, ''that we have so little time in which to simply enjoy what's around us. Or maybe I should say, *I* take too little time.''

''That's too bad,'' she said, although lately the same was true for her. ''It really is beautiful today, isn't it?''

''It is. No matter how busy I get today, I want to remain aware of that. I think we lose something important when we're not in touch with our environment. Is that me? I sound like a philosopher today.''

''That's all right. Some days are like that.''

As they neared the bridge, Kara cast aside all thought

of keeping the conversation focused on her father. She'd left two messages for him on his machine last night, but either he hadn't been home or the tone of her voice had warned him that she might tell him something he didn't want to know.

By the time she stirred herself, Brand was already at work. Under his and Chuck's direction, all the old wood was removed and piled up where a couple of the men could begin sawing them into lengths that would fit in Cliff's and Ada's wood stove. Once the work area was clean, the new timbers were wrapped with chains and jockeyed around, with the help of a winch on one of the men's trucks, until they spanned the creek. Between the sound of machinery and barked directions, Kara could barely get Ada and Cliff to hear a word she had to say. She finally persuaded them to sit in a couple of lawn chairs with her. Her muscles needed exercise and she chafed because she wasn't out there helping, but if she left Cliff and Ada, that would set them apart from everyone else— single them out as being too old to work. She wouldn't do that to them.

From her vantage point, she kept her eye both on the work and the thin wisps of clouds that occasionally skittered across the sky. From time to time she reached down to pat Mooch who, when he wasn't getting in the way, slept at her feet. When Chuck's girlfriend arrived, she stopped by long enough to introduce herself, then went to work.

"Isn't this wonderful," Ada yelled at her. "To be able to watch other folks work. Like you said, someone's got to supervise. It's a hell of a job, but I think I'm up to it. I don't suppose they'd take too kindly to it if I cracked a whip. Just for the fun of it."

"I wouldn't recommend it." The supporting timbers were now in place and cross lumber was being nailed to that. Although there were any number of things to look at, Kara's attention was continually drawn to Brand. Much of what he did on the mountain was of a supervisory nature—out of necessity. Here was different; here he was just another strong arm. Whether he was balancing himself on a log or driving in nails, every movement he made was graceful. From what her brother had told her, she knew he'd been several feet above the ground when the collapse in Anchorage happened. A less athletic man wouldn't have been able to scramble free. He might even have been killed.

The thought made her shiver despite the day's warmth. She had to concentrate on the sun on her back for several minutes before the feeling went away. Still, she was left with a deep thankfulness that the worst hadn't happened.

And thank God Brand hadn't been crippled at nineteen. How different his life would have been!

Early in the afternoon, she and Ada went back to the house to get started on the meal they'd promised the workers. They were close to finishing the bridge and sure to be hungry. Although Kara suggested that Cliff might want to join them, he informed them that he was too busy to be wasting time in the kitchen. When he agreed to stay where he was and keep an eye on Mooch, she left, after getting him to promise that he'd give her a blow by blow of what was being done.

She felt out of her element seasoning hamburgers to feed ten hungry men and women. This domestic role was a new one for her, but if she'd stayed at the work site, Ada would have had to do the work alone. And she would have had to go on looking at Brand, thinking about how close he'd come to disaster.

That's what she had to get across to her father, why she wanted to get his approval to talk openly and honestly to Brand.

She was grateful for the interruption to her thoughts when the crew finally trooped into the house, complaining that they hadn't eaten in days. She thought she'd seen hearty eaters in her life, but this bunch must have been starved for a homecooked meal.

"Cliff's never eaten like that," Ada confided as she watched her husband pile his plate with baked beans and a massive hamburger. She stared at her own mounded plate. "Me either, and, between you and me, I've put away a few boarding house meals in my life." She patted her broad hips to get her point across. "Are you sure we have enough potato salad?"

Because she and Ada had stayed up late last night preparing the salad, Kara wasn't worried about that. "Just don't tell them there's still more in my refrigerator," she said in a conspiratoral whisper. "Otherwise, they might never leave."

Her words came back to haunt her several times during the afternoon when it seemed as if no one had anywhere else to go and nothing to do but play horseshoes and talk about what a great job they'd done. Finally, however, the crew started wandering away, still talking about how hard they'd worked and how good the meal had been.

Soon only Chuck and his girlfriend and Brand were left. Brand explained that cement had been used as part of the bridge's base and until that had had a couple of days to set, they shouldn't put any heavy weight on the structure. "You can walk on it, but I wouldn't bring any vehicles over it." He rubbed his flat stomach and grinned like a satisfied cat. "Are you sure there's nothing else we can do? If you promise to feed us like that again, it wouldn't take much to get everyone back."

"We can't afford to put on another spread," Ada pointed out. "Oh, we appreciated it no end, but—" She ended with a yawn.

"I was just joking," Brand informed her. "The way you provided for this gang went way beyond the call of duty. I'm afraid you let yourself get too tired. My mom hates admitting it, but she just can't do holiday meals the way she used to."

"Yeah. I know. Getting old's the pits."

When Kara glanced over at Cliff in his rocking chair, she saw he was asleep. In a quiet voice, she asked Ada if maybe he needed to go to bed. Ada explained that Cliff often took naps there and had never fallen out. "He hasn't had that much excitement in lord knows how long. Me either."

Chuck had gotten to his feet and was heading toward the door. Rubbing his stomach in imitation of what Brand had done, the other hand around his girlfriend's shoulder, he announced that they were on their way. As he spoke, he kept his eyes on Brand, but if he was trying to hint that it was time for Brand to leave as well, Brand missed the point. Either that, Kara thought, or he was ignoring the message.

Standing, Brand walked over to her and held out his hand. For a moment she simply looked at it, struck by its competence and strength. Then she placed hers in it and allowed him to help her to her feet. "Let's let Cliff and Ada get some rest," he suggested. Before giving her a chance to say anything, he steered her outside.

She stepped out onto the porch and waited. Thin fingers of clouds continued to paint the sky, but it was still blue, still looked as if it went on forever. She thought Brand might want her to go with him so they could look at the bridge one last time before he left. Instead, he started walking toward her cabin. She followed, curious, only a little uneasy.

He opened the door and stepped inside the cool, quiet interior. By the time she entered, he was heading to the couch. With a grunt, he settled himself on it and looked up at her from under heavy lids. He patted the space beside him.

"Tell me about your father."

Kara could have sworn the room tilted. She reached out for something to hold onto and found only air. "My father?"

"You were talking about him earlier today. We got sidetracked."

"Oh." Barely aware of what she was doing, she sat down. Still, she kept herself alert. "I'm surprised you remembered."

"He sounds like a man I'd like. Obviously he's had a great influence on your life."

Like? Kara fingered her necklace, then glanced down at the tiny ring. "He has," she said, her voice firm. "He's the reason I'm in this business." She had to be careful not too say too much. Otherwise, she might give something away, and today, feeling as she did about being with Brand, wasn't the time.

"Then he's in construction."

"He semi-retired now." *Liar. Her father wasn't working at what he loved because, in part, of what Brand had done.* "Still, I can't see him ever getting away from construction, not if there's any way he can prevent it."

"Prevent? What makes you say that?"

Kara felt as if she was walking on the edge of a cliff. A wrong movement and—"I was just talking. Too tired to listen to what I'm saying."

"Are you?"

She shrugged elaborately, pretended to yawn, then cast around for something to say. "I don't think Cliff's ever had more fun. I'm sure it meant a lot to him to have you ask his advice the way you did."

Brand threw her a look that lasted longer than she wanted it to. Obviously he hadn't bought her attempt at changing the subject. Still, she knew what she had to do. She made herself settle back against the couch and yawned elaborately. "Between you and me, I hope Cliff and Ada don't have any more major projects. I'd like to relax a little on my next day off.''

"So would I. With you."

Don't do this to me. I don't know what to say. "I suppose we could," she said casually when she didn't feel that way at all. His aftershave hadn't survived the day. Now the impact was earthy, strongly male. "That exploring you mentioned the other day."

"Exploring." Brand drew out the word. Then, before she could prepare herself for it, he reached out, took her hand, and held it in front of him. In the dim light she wasn't sure what he might see. He ran a fingernail over her mother's ring, then glanced at her cameo necklace. Finally he met her eyes. "There are so many contrasts to you. When I see you working, I think there isn't anything you can't do. But the jewelry—it brings out another side. A basic femininity."

She didn't say anything; not a single word formed inside her mind.

"Does my saying that bother you?"

"No." With her free hand, she fingered her necklace. "Not really. I am what I am. I've—" she worked up a smile, "gotten to that point in my life where fitting into any kind of a mold simply doesn't concern me. Old and opinionated, Ada calls it."

"It's a good place to be, most of the time."

She heard his words, and yet she didn't. What she was aware of was the lilt, the timbre of his voice. As for what he was trying to say, she could only wait and hope that her ability to concentrate improved.

"You don't know what I'm talking about, do you?"

"No. I'm sorry. I—"

He exhaled; the effort took a long time. "I'm thinking I need to tell you some things about myself. About where I'm coming from and why, maybe, you'd want to end things here and now."

"End?"

"I'm not always an easy man to be around."

He'd held onto her hand, cradling it lightly in his palm. She gave a half thought to freeing herself, but he'd begun to surround her, take her over the way a hard driving piece of music did when the mood was right—like the other night, in his arms.

"I'm not an easy woman to be around," she gave back. "I'm not what a lot of men want, what they expect a woman to be. I've never had a manicure, that kind of thing."

He touched the tip of a nail. "Then those men are fools. Kara, I hardly know how to say this, and I don't know whether you want to hear it."

"I can't say unless you tell me something."

"True. I guess what I'm getting at is, I can be damn singleminded when it comes to something I believe in. Maybe I shouldn't be that dogged; I'll probably live longer if I'm not. But when I see something that needs doing, or believe needs doing, I sink my teeth into it. I don't know any other way of being. Do you know what I'm saying?"

She did. More than he could possibly understand. Instead of telling him that, she rested her head against the back of the couch and closed her eyes. The gesture drew her away from him and he released her hand. Still, she felt the warmth of his shoulder against hers.

She wanted to stay like that until tomorrow. Wanted to listen to the humming inside her body.

"Maybe that's what it takes to succeed in one's own business," she told him. "To know when you have to put professional goals ahead of a personal life."

"Yes."

Yes. It was such a simple word, and yet because she was tuned in to him, she understood the full impact behind it. Brand Lockwood had put certain things in his own life on the back burner because he believed in his ability to make his mark on the world, because he'd set certain goals for himself and those goals meant everything to him. Maybe that was why he hadn't married, yet.

"I can't say whether that's wise or not," she told him. "Whether people should be singleminded, driven. But if you have a dream, a goal, I'm not sure you have a choice. It comes first. It consumes you."

He didn't say anything. She thought about opening her eyes to see if he was looking at her, but she sensed he was. Maybe that meant that with her words she'd touched the core of what he was as a human being. She wanted to believe that. "I have a friend, a beautiful woman who could probably make a fortune as a model," she went on. "But the only thing Cathy really wants out of life is to write. To write and have people be touched by what she has to say. I don't know whether she'll ever make it to the top, but I think she might because that one goal is more important than anything else in her life. Her life isn't balanced, but she doesn't care."

"What's your goal?"

For several seconds she tried to put the words together, but she found herself thinking about him—about his broad, warm shoulder, the slow, deep rising and falling of his chest. Even with her eyes closed, she was able to picture his thick, dark hair and the way the wind took claim of it. She'd never seen him in anything except faded jeans and shirts that emphasized his breadth.

He'd come into the cabin with her. She'd sat down beside him. And, right or wrong, she would stay as long as the challenge, the danger that radiated out of him, touched her.

Mountain man. Maybe that's what he was.

When, caught in the weave of her thoughts, she opened her eyes, she saw him as a dark, indistinct blur that took up her world. Maybe she should have felt uneasy about that, but she didn't. Tomorrow she'd think about the consequences of their being together.

Tonight she'd be with him.

He was looking at her strangely. She'd never answered his question. "My goal?" she said. The word rang inside her; she gave it meaning. "To be part of creating something that will outlast me and yet leave the environment as untouched as possible. I think I'd like to be involved in formulating zoning laws someday, to be in on the decision making when it comes to determining quality of life. Maybe this sounds hokey, but I'd like to help build truly affordable housing for those who otherwise wouldn't have a home." She stopped, awed by the task she'd given herself. "Short term, I need to pay my bills."

He laughed a little at that. Then, eyes becoming smokey, he placed his arm around her shoulder and slowly drew her close. "What about your private life?"

She was glad he felt comfortable enough around her to ask. Still, the question demanded a great deal from her. "I want children, someday. A—" No. She didn't want to waffle on this. "A man in my life who shares the same goals and dreams."

"What about a house in the suburbs? Credit cards?"

Through indistinct vision, she took in what she could see of her surroundings. "I've helped build houses. I've never really had that much of a desire to put down roots in one."

"Neither have I."

She turned to look at him, but because she couldn't bring anything into focus, she could only guess at his mood. "Where do you live?"

"Nowhere, really. I always rent when I'm on a job. I have an answering service, a post office box in Seattle. Like I said, my career takes up a huge chunk of my life."

So has mine. "Do you ever regret that?"

He hadn't stopped gazing at her. "I don't often think about that. Maybe."

There was a great deal more she could ask him, but the questions swirled, unformed, inside her and she couldn't pull them together. She wanted to tell him that she'd never expected to respect him, but it had happened.

She couldn't.

Driven by a need she refused to analyze, she reached out through the mist that was her world and found Brand's cheek with her fingertips. There was nothing soft about his flesh, but she wouldn't have it otherwise. She didn't remember willing her fingers to trace the tiny lines at the corner of his eyes, but they were there, and she was learning even more about Brand Lockwood. He'd been hardened by the world he'd chosen to work and live in. The wind and rain and sun should have sanded him away until nothing was left. But there, under that first strong layer, was his beating pulse. The channel to his heart.

His arm around her tightened. He pulled her closer until she could no longer see anything except dark shadows. Giving up, she closed her eyes and simply felt. Simply experienced.

When he breathed, she breathed with him. Maybe she could hear his heart; maybe she only imagined it. But she couldn't deny the direction her own heart wanted to take. Blindly, she sought his lips and found them ready for her. Their first touch was simply that, a gentle meeting between two people who shouldn't still be strangers but were because one carried secrets inside her.

Then he became more than that.

Growing more sure of herself, she wrapped her arms around his neck and held on. She felt his tongue darting out to press past her strangely slack lips. She went with the movement, losing herself in the little piece of himself he'd given her. An instant ago she'd been asking herself if she was truly insane to be sitting here with him.

She no longer asked.

Inside, she began to soften, to feel as if she'd been touched by something hot and alive. Still pressed against him, she tried to pull in enough air to clear her head. Then, before her lungs had filled, she no longer cared.

If she was going to lose herself in Brand, so be it.

Greedy now, she pressed her finger against the back of his neck, tapping the corded strength there. His energy arched out to touch a like emotion in her. Her breasts became full, heavy. Deep inside, her body knotted, feeling as if it had been touched with molten lava.

Unable to stop herself now, she turned her head to one side and sucked in oxygen. She thought he was doing the same thing, but before she could be sure, his hand was at her throat, inching lower. Pressing past buttons and bra and covering the swell of her breast. She arched herself, giving him easy access, now gripping his upper arms with fingers that bit down and held.

She felt a forefinger on the tip of her breast, pushing in, bringing it to life. *Let him know—everything.*

Instead, she slid her fingers beneath his shirt and pressed against the warm mountain of his chest. Once his heat had flowed into her, she ran her hand lower, felt his stomach muscles tighten and hold.

"Kara?"

Kara, what?

"We're playing with fire."

I know that.

"Did you hear me, we're—"

"I know." *How I know.* He'd cradled her breast in the palm of his hand, making a lie of his warning.

"We aren't ready."

She was aware of that, far better than he could possibly be. Still, instinct had taken over and she couldn't begin to think how to free herself. *I don't care,* she wanted to tell him, but enough sanity remained that she knew she'd always regret it if they became lovers tonight.

"Right." With an awful wrench, she pulled herself free. When she looked down at herself, she was surprised to realize that he'd unfastened all of her buttons. Her breasts still felt too large for her bra.

His gaze settled on her there, then, slowly, he lifted his head and met her eyes. "I think I'd better go."

"Yes." She thought about getting to her feet and walking away but couldn't remember how to make her legs support her. "Yes. I think you should."

SEVEN

If Brand had asked her why she'd decided to walk out to his truck with him, she wouldn't have been able to give him an answer. Given what nearly happened between them, she should have stayed behind.

But she hadn't because she hadn't wanted the evening, with him, to end.

"It's a professional-looking job," she said of the newly finished bridge. "It'll probably last longer than either the cabin or Cliff and Ada's house."

"I was thinking the same thing, but don't tell Cliff. To hear him, you'd think that cabin he and his brother built is destined to become as much of a landmark as the Mascot Saloon."

"Let's not disillusion him. This is between the two of us?"

"Our secret."

Brand had held her hand during the walk out. The contact was casual, light, with none of the sensual impact she'd felt when they were in each other's arms. She thought, not about his words, but how she'd gone from wanting to make love to him to simply wanting to be in his presence. That's what held her, the contrasts. The fascinating complexity of him—and her need to understand that complexity.

"The bridge went in so quickly," she said. "I think that's what really got to them. That and the way everyone worked together. I don't know if I said thank you, but I want to. What you did for them was wonderful."

"I enjoyed it, Kara. It felt good, very good, to be able to help them."

Help. That was the kind of man he was. For her father's sake, she needed him to be hard and uncaring. For herself—no. What she needed wasn't important. "Well . . ." She looked around at her surroundings, the trees dancing with the wind, the sky painted with endlessly darkening streaks of rose and blue/black, Brand, warm and caring, beside her. "This is as far as I go. I'll see you tomorrow."

"Early, unfortunately." She expected him to release her. Instead, he turned so he was facing her, looking down at her. In an instant, she no longer felt casual or relaxed. She didn't fight the change. Couldn't begin to fight whatever had claimed her with nothing more than a glance. "What we did a few minutes ago—" he said. "I'm sorry. It happened too fast. I think we'd both agree on that. But, unless you tell me not to see you again, it—whatever that is—isn't going to end with tonight."

Oh Brand. If—when—I tell you certain things, you won't want anything to do with me. You'll hate me. "I don't know what you want me to say."

"Don't you? Kara, I've told you. There hasn't been much time in my life for long-term relationships. I'm ready for that to change. What I feel when we're together is something I want to explore."

With me? No. "Do you?"

"Yes. I do. That night down by the dock, you shared some of your dreams with me. I've seen the way you stand up for yourself. You know who you are, what you want out of life. I see myself in the same way." His frown pulled his eyes into shadow. "Something is happening between us. I want to explore it. With you. It shouldn't be hard for you to tell me whether you feel the same way."

She couldn't go on looking at him, couldn't go on keeping the truth from him. The lie had stretched out long enough and now, somehow, despite the promise her father had tried to wrestle out of her . . . "No. It shouldn't," she whispered. "Or it wouldn't be if . . ."

With his free hand, he cupped her chin and forced her to meet his gaze. "If what? Kara, what is this about?"

What? She desperately wanted to be thinking, saying anything except this. But she'd flown to Skagway, Alaska, because she needed the truth. Coming to respect and care about Brand Lockwood complicated things in ways she'd never dreamed possible. He'd wanted to make love to her. He had to know she'd wanted the same thing. If she went on deceiving him, he would hate her later even more than he would now.

This way was better, in truth the only way.

"It's about who I am."

"You're a competent professional and a beautiful woman."

She shook her head. Had anything been harder than this? But, she knew, she couldn't do anything else. Not if she wanted to face herself. And she did; she had to. "I appreciate the compliment, but, Brand—you know my married name is Richardson, but my maiden name . . ." Oh, God, how was she going to say this?

There was only one way. Drawing away from him, she met his dark eyes. "Art Crayton is my father."

He rocked backward; his features instantly contorted as if she'd struck him. "Crayton?"

"I never—never thought I'd have to tell you like this. That you and I . . ."

"Art Crayton is your father?"

Had she shocked him that much? She must have. "I wish—" No. She'd never wish she hadn't been born a Crayton. "I can't get my father to tell me anything. Do you have any idea how hard that's been for me, not knowing? His pride—I'm not sure of all his reasons. Whatever they are, I can't break through them. But—" Feeling her nails bite into her palms, she felt stronger. "I also can't sit back and do nothing, know nothing. My father needs my brother and me by his side, even if he thinks he has to go it alone."

"Let him."

"No," she returned the challenge. "I can't. I won't. You were there. You know what happened that day."

"Yeah. I do."

She felt as if she'd been speared by his gaze. Still, she stood her ground. "Then you know a thousand times more than what I do."

"And that's why you're here? To drag out of me what you can't get from your father?"

His words sounded dead. She couldn't tell anything from his tone of voice. "That and because, right now, I'm the only means of support my family has."

"I see."

Although there were any number of things she could say or try to say, she waited him out. She sensed that he was still trying to recover from what she'd told him. She'd give him time to accept what neither of them could change. She owed him that.

And then she'd deal with his reaction.

Because she couldn't go on looking at him, she wandered away and stepped onto the bridge. She stood in the endless dusk, remembering how hard Brand had worked that day, how they'd laughed and joked together, how much pleasure he'd gotten from seeing the gratitude on Cliff's and Ada's faces when the job was done.

Most of all she remembered what it felt like to be in his arms. To want him as much as he wanted her.

"Why didn't you tell me earlier?"

"Why?" She kept her back to him. "Because I was afraid you'd fire me."

"Were you? What would you have done if I'd sent you packing?"

"Gone home. What else could I do?" They were so far apart. It was better this way, and yet she wanted to be close enough that she might pick up on his emotion. Now she could only concentrate on his words. "You hold all the bargaining chips, Brand."

"I didn't know we were bargaining."

"This—this way—isn't what I want. But it has to be." She hated the desperation in her voice, but she didn't know how to erase it. "Brand, from the moment of the collapse, my father has shut himself off from me. He'll hardly talk to me, and not about what we need to. He ordered me not to tell you who I am. I thought, I guess I thought I could respect his request. That my love for him would bind me. But I can't do that." *I look at you and can't be anything except honest.*

"It's hard for me to respect a man like that."

"Stop it!" She whirled toward him. Her body felt so taut that she wasn't sure she could take a single step. "You think he's some kind of monster, don't you?"

"His negligence nearly killed me. And his son."

If she wrapped her arms around her middle he would know how deeply he'd wounded her. Only, she couldn't help herself. "He's never been negligent in his life."

"Hasn't he?" He threw the words at her. "A whole damn structure went down. A structure your father was responsible for. Kara, your brother was almost killed. The investigation—"

"What about the investigation?" She ground out the words. "That's the hell of it. My father won't tell me anything and I can't get anyone involved to answer my calls. That leaves you.''

"So you came up here and threw yourself at me hoping I'd tell you everything.''

She gripped her middle even tighter and began rocking herself. "I did *not* throw myself at you,'' she whispered through her pain. "We both know that. I'm being honest with you tonight, aren't I? I'm breaking my word with my father because I can't deceive you—because you mean too much to me for that.''

Two minutes ago Brand had wanted to walk away from her, never wanted to see her again. But he couldn't ignore the pain in her voice or her body telling him how much he'd hurt her. Or the voice inside him. Strangely, he wanted to ask her to forgive him. But he didn't. "I suppose I should tell you I respect you for that.''

"I don't care.'' She pulled one hand off her waist and raked it through her hair. It was still light; he glimpsed raw agony in her eyes. That tore at him almost as much as learning who she was.

"You don't care what?'' he asked.

"Whether you respect or hate me.''

He didn't believe that—didn't want to. She didn't give him time to tell her that. "All I want is honesty in return,'' she went on. "In a little while I'm going to have to call my father and tell him what I've just done. Will I also have to tell him that it all blew up in my face? That you told me this is between you and the professionals involved and I have no business, no right, knowing why you were there that day, what you've said, what you suspect. That you've fired me?''

He'd told her he'd never fire her. Was that why she'd brought up the subject again, because she was that afraid? What was it she'd said? That she'd taken this job because she had to support her father and brother. He had to admire her for that.

He also couldn't forget that she'd waited until she'd taken their relationship beyond professional and into personal before telling him the truth.

"My father's a good man, Brand," she said in a tone he could do nothing but respect. "I know you don't believe that. You wouldn't have gone to the investigators if you thought different. But you're wrong."

"Am I?"

"Yes! He raised two children alone, built his business one step at a time, gave employment to hundreds of men over the years, helped—"

"That's only part of it."

She stood with her mouth open and her body so rigid he thought she might shatter. "Go on," she challenged. "What is the rest of it? That's what I came here to find out."

Less than an hour ago he'd come within a breath of telling her he wanted to make love to her. She'd pulled back; he'd pulled back. And now with her revelation, she'd destroyed his desire for her.

Most of his desire.

He slid his hands in his back pockets to keep them from reaching for her. "It's been turned over to the investigators, Kara. The decision is out of both of our hands."

"I know that. What did you tell them? That's what I need to know—for my father's sake. So I can be there for him. Do I have to beg, Brand? What's it going to take?"

With those few words she'd laid herself open to him. She couldn't get the truth from her father for reasons known only to Art Crayton, and that hurt her, deeply. Brand could see that. He'd tell her what happened. He owed her that. But it wouldn't be tonight, when he couldn't look at her without being reminded of his hands on her breasts, kisses that made him hungry for more.

He joined her on the bridge, being careful to keep from getting too close to her. He felt her tension. It seeped into him and blocked him from the other things he needed to be thinking about. "Thank you." He spoke through lips that didn't want to move.

Her head snapped back. "For what?"

"For being honest. Before our relationship went too far."

Although she didn't move, he knew he'd hurt her. He didn't care—he didn't want to care. "It would have been a hell of a lot harder if we'd become lovers."

When she stared at him, he saw, not anger as he wanted, but even more hurt. Then she blinked. When she opened her eyes again he knew she had her pain under control. "That's why I said what I did," she said. "So I wouldn't regret any more of this than I already do."

Damn. He didn't want to admire her, and certainly not this much, but how could he feel anything else? He should leave; he knew that. The turning and walking away was maybe the hardest thing he'd ever done.

"Wait."

Her whispered command stopped him. Because he didn't trust himself to look at her again, he stood with his back to her, waiting.

"You haven't told me anything." She hadn't gotten her voice above a whisper.

"I know," he said, hating himself when his anger should be directed at her for putting him in this position. For being who she was? "But this is all I can deal with right now. You're going to have to wait."

"How long?"

"Not long. I'll tell you everything—unlike your father."

"Brand?"

He counted, one, two, three.

"Do you want me on the mountain tomorrow?"

"Yes." The word came out slowly, painfully, honestly. "Yes."

*　　*　　*

At least he hadn't fired her. And given what she'd told him, how could she ask for anything more?

The truth, Kara acknowledged as she made her slow way back to Cliff and Ada's house for the phone call she had to make. What was so damn hard about that? If she could travel hundreds of miles and face him, why couldn't he give her that?

Because this wasn't any easier for him than it was for her?

Maybe.

Cliff was already snoring in the bedroom when Ada answered her knock on the door, but Ada assured her that she was free to use the phone. Although Ada kept looking at her, she couldn't bring herself to tell the other woman why she probably looked as if she'd been punched in the stomach.

After five rings, Hank picked up the phone. "Sorry," he said breathlessly. "I was outside."

"How are you getting around?"

"It's better every day. I'm going to be back at work sooner than those pessimistic therapists think I am. At least one thing's going right. What are you up to?"

Making a mess of my life. "Not much. Is Dad there?"

"He's asleep, sis. He has been since a little after dinner."

Kara leaned against the wall, staring absently at Ada. "Dad? But he's a night owl."

"Not recently. He's been sleeping a lot. And I think he's having some pretty bad dreams. He's only putting in a few hours a day doing that consulting work, but it wears him out."

"Oh, no. Has he gone back to a doctor?"

"That hardhead, are you kidding? I brought it up yesterday for the umpteenth time and he just about bit my head off. I can't tie the old goat up and force him to do something he doesn't want to. You know that as well as I do."

"Yes. Unfortunately, I do," she said around the worry that nagged at her and stripped her mind of what she'd felt when Brand drove away without looking back at her. "Look, I'll try to reach him after work tomorrow. Tell him that, will you? There's something he has to know."

"What something?"

"I—I told Brand who I am."

Hank let out his breath. "And?"

"And it's uncomfortable."

"I bet it is. He hasn't given you your walking papers?"

"No." Relief spread through her, easing a little of the strain. "He also hasn't told me what we need to know."

"Damn. Because it's hush-hush?"

"No. I'm sure that's not it." She pressed two fingers against the bridge of her nose. Somewhere beyond her reach a headache had taken root. Then, keeping her voice to a whisper, she explained that Brand had promised to answer her questions, soon.

"In the meantime you tiptoe around him."

"Something like that." Her headache increased. "Look, you'll tell Dad I called, won't you? I'm not asking you to do my dirty work for me. I'll tell him what happened as soon as I can—unless, unless you think it wouldn't be good for his health."

"None of what's happening is good for his health, sis. I can't see how anything you say will make it worse than it already is."

Feeling as if he'd spent the night on a bar stool instead of stretched out in bed staring at the ceiling, Brand parked his pickup where he always did at the work site and went in search of Chuck. Chuck's girlfriend had to return to her job in Seattle today. Consequently, Brand hadn't seen anything of his roommate last night, not that he'd been in any shape for conversation.

He found his foreman by his own rig, staring at blueprints that kept trying to roll back up. After a short discussion about how to deal with yet another unstable slope, the men went their separate ways.

Yesterday's clear weather had given way to thick, heavy clouds that seemed tailormade for Brand's mood. He pulled his shirt collar up around his neck, cursed the stiff wind that swirled dust in all directions, and glanced around at what he was creating.

He felt awed, both by nature's immensity and the small, competent woman who easily controlled tons of machinery and looked at home on a mountain that had brought gold seekers to their knees.

Today she wore an oversized sweatshirt. If he didn't know what she looked and felt like under all that bulk, he might have been fooled into believing there was more to her than there was. But he'd spent the night trying to forget that very body. Because the attempt had been a dismal failure, he recalled every line, every curve. Although the sweatshirt hugged her throat, he had no doubt that she wore her mother's necklace. Today she'd want that comforting presence more than usual. If he took her hand, he'd feel the delicate silver that circled her little finger, a ring so simple and uncluttered that she dared wear it around machinery.

Simple. Uncluttered. That's what he wanted in the way of a relationship with her.

Tough. He wasn't going to get it.

You're going to have to wait, he told her. Why? Because he didn't have the guts to tell her what he suspected about her father? Hardly. Then what?

Halfway through the question, he found himself staring the answer in the face. He'd put her off last night because he didn't want them to be any more at loggerheads than they already were, and because he didn't want her to tell him he had no business believing her father was incompetent or dishonest or both. But mostly he'd remained silent because he didn't want to hurt her.

Hurt her. If she didn't mean anything to him, he wouldn't care.

After a few more seconds, he lowered his head against the churning dust and approached her. She sat waiting for him in the high cab, the bulldozer rumbling, vibrating her small form. Because he didn't want anyone to hear what he had to say to her, he hoisted himself into the cab and stood over her. When she looked up at him, he followed the taut line of her throat. He'd been right. She was wearing the dainty cameo. "It's time," he said, wishing to hell he was better at this kind of thing.

"Time." She licked her lips, drawing his attention to the fact that she hadn't worn makeup this morning. He suspected it was because what they'd said and done last night had distracted her from her usual routine. Without that touch of shadow and mascara she looked less finished, even more vulnerable.

"Not now," he thought to say. "This evening after work."

"All right." She blinked but went on looking at him. "I tried to reach my dad. He deserves to know what's going on. But he was asleep. Hank says he's tired all the time. That scares me."

He didn't care about that. Or maybe the truth was, he didn't want to care. Either way, he couldn't completely distance himself from what she would have to go through with her father. "I'll take you out to dinner. We'll talk then." His invitation stopped him. Until he heard himself say the words, he'd had no idea that was what he was going to suggest.

"You don't have to do that."

"Yeah. I think maybe I do."

By the time work was over, Kara's stomach was tied

in such a knot she wasn't sure she'd be able to drink water, let alone eat. She'd managed a bite of her lunch but had to stop when she began to feel queasy. She left her sandwich on a rock, hoping at least someone would benefit from her uneaten meal. Before she'd taken more than a dozen steps, Stella's wild dog had swooped down on it. She'd watched the animal wheel and trot away, wishing he'd stay so she could talk to him.

Enough, she told herself as she headed down the mountain. Damn it, she'd known it wouldn't be easy when she made the decision to try to wrestle information from Brand Lockwood. Back then, she'd told herself she'd survive whatever she learned and use that knowledge to help her father fight to salvage his career—despite Brand.

But now a new element had been added: the way she felt about Brand.

When that element followed her to the cabin and sat on her shoulder while she changed into clothes that weren't dust coated, she faced it squarely. She cared for Brand, respected and admired him. She felt the same way about her father. Reconciling those emotions wouldn't be easy. Her task—impossible task—was to survive an insane balancing act.

Still, as she turned off the light and closed the door behind her, she was glad Brand had waited outside. She slipped into his truck without saying a word and paid scant attention as he drove into town. He parked to the side of the historic Ivory Inn. "Chuck's eaten here a couple of times," Brand said. "He raves about their stew and sourdough bread."

"That sounds fine." She opened her door and stepped down out of the cab. He followed her into the inn, keeping enough distance between them that she shouldn't be aware of his presence. They were seated at a small window table with high-backed chairs and a deep red tablecloth. Small lamps with red shades on each table provided the only artificial light. From what she could tell, the inn appeared filled with visitors. Good. She didn't want anyone they knew interrupting them.

When Brand picked up the oversized menu, she did the same. But although she tried to concentrate, she couldn't make sense of the selections. When the waitress came to take their order, she asked for the house special, not caring what they brought her. Brand ordered the same.

Finally she took a sip of the wine he'd chosen and faced him. In the muted light, his features had taken on a deep red hue. Much of his face was cast in shadow, which had the effect of erasing his hard edges, leaving him more illusion than reality.

"I want to tell you more about my father," she began. She waited, wondering if he might tell her he wasn't interested. He said nothing. "Not about the business part of him, although that's important, too." She placed her elbows on the table. The gesture brought her closer to him. Still, she couldn't tell what was going on inside him. Would she ever again, or had he learned how to block her off from his emotions?

"I'm listening."

How long had she been silent? With an effort, she concentrated. "Brand, I was eight when my mother died. Hank wasn't even in school yet. At the time of her death, Dad was off on a construction job. I don't know what he was doing when he got the news; that time isn't something he likes to talk about. He flew home, handled the details of the funeral, gave notice to the landlord, took me out of school, and flew Hank and me back to the job with him. He did all that in a week."

Caught up in memories, she went on. "I remember the look on his face when he walked in the door and took me in his arms. I'd always thought of my father as a giant, the strongest, most confident man in the world. But that day he looked old and scared and so full of grief. He cried;

I'd never seen him cry before. That's when I realized he was human and not the superman his eight-year-old daughter had made him.''

She took another sip of wine. A couple with a baby walked past but she didn't take her eyes off Brand. "I'm seeing the same look on his face these days," she said around the tears that threatened to get in the way of what she had to say. "Old and scared. That's why I did what I did—because I can't let him go through this alone. When Mom died, I couldn't be the support he needed. It's different now.''

"I understand.''

Did he? Fighting down the wash of emotion that went with his simple words, she went on. "He wasn't a perfect parent; he couldn't be both father and mother. There were certain things, traditional feminine things, that he didn't know how to tell me about. His jobs required that we moved a lot. The teachers were always telling him that our education would suffer, although I don't agree. Besides, that's the way things were. We simply played the hand we were dealt.''

She'd already been speaking softly, but her voice lowered even more. "From him, Hank and I learned the most important things—how to exist as a unit. We loved and respected each other. All that moving taught me tolerance for other life-styles. I learned what it took to feel connected with a new community in a short time, how to quickly make friends, and how to put those friendships behind me when the time for moving came again.'' She stared into her drink, seeing—seeing what? "I also picked up a strong work ethic from my father.''

She couldn't think of anything else to say. There were a thousand details, stories of how Art Crayton had helped his children with their homework, gone into clothing stores with his maturing daughter, consoled her through teenage broken hearts, but emotion was so tightly woven around the words that she couldn't separate one from the other. She wasn't ready to reveal that much of herself.

Brand was still watching her, whatever emotion was in his eyes shielded by red-tinged shadows. She kept her fingers wrapped around her wine glass but didn't take another drink.

"Your teachers were wrong."

"What?"

"Your teachers. When they said your education would suffer with all that moving, they didn't know what they were talking about."

"I know." She went on looking at him, trying to make sense of his tone. But, caught up in her own thoughts, she found that nearly impossible. "Dad didn't finish high school because he had to go to work. He's never said too much about that, just that he did what he had to. A few years later he got his GED. He's taken a number of college courses, all related to his business. He's always said he didn't really understand what schools had to offer until Hank and I were students, and until they offered something he could put to practical use."

Brand nodded. The gesture took his features out of the shadows and for a moment she read what was in his eyes. He wasn't condemning; he hadn't made any judgment. Instead, he simply listened. "So you don't have any regrets about the way you were raised. But if you could have had it your way, you wouldn't have spent your growing up years moving around, would you?" he asked.

"I wouldn't have chosen to lose my mother. We take what life dishes out."

He thought to tell her that having been raised by a man might have forged her in many ways, but it hadn't stripped an ingrained femininity from her. She'd freed her dark hair. It flowed around her, framing and gentling her. She'd changed into a pale yellow sweater with a wide neck that accented the cameo at her throat. The red hues cast by the lamp reflected off the tiny ring she wore and made the fingers around her wine glass look less substantial than they did by day. But if he told her those things, she would know too much about him.

Damn it, he didn't want to care about her father. On that fateful day in Anchorage, Art Crayton had simply been a stubborn old man who refused to listen, to admit he hadn't kept abreast of technology. He'd had nothing but contempt for Art then. Then.

"Kara?" He waited until he was sure he had her full attention. "You wanted to know what happened between your father and me. Why I'd gone to see him and what he said to me."

She said nothing.

"That's why you came looking for me, isn't it?" His question sounded hard-edged. He was instantly sorry but didn't know how to change things.

"Yes."

Yes. Wasn't she going to give him anything more than that? "That's what we're here for, isn't it?"

"Yes. I don't know what else to say."

"I guess there isn't anything else." He'd finished his wine. When had that happened? "All right. I'd recently heard of a new kind of polymer which doubles the strength of cement. I'd tested it myself so I knew the claims weren't exaggerated. The bottom line, a mere eight percent more than the usual cost of cement. That's what I wanted to tell your dad about. He wasn't interested."

"Doubles?" she repeated in disbelief.

She looked wounded. If he said more, he'd only increase her pain, but she'd asked for this. "The product has been used in France for years. Just because our government hasn't made its use a requirement here is no reason for builders not to take advantage of the technology— especially in areas with a high earthquake potential. That's what I said, tried to say, to your father."

He paused as their waitress brought salad, then went on without first taking a bite. "Your dad agreed that Alaska is earthquake prone, but he didn't want to hear what I had to say."

He watched, both fascinated and wary, as she straightened her spine. "I find that hard to believe."

All right, so he'd altered the story slightly. But surely she understood that the end result had been the same. "He heard me out. I'll give him that. But when I was done, he said that not only couldn't he hold up construction long enough to order the polymer, but that it would take him over budget. Since his bid had already been accepted, he'd wind up in the red."

"Of course he would. You know how small the margin of profit is. But you didn't buy his explanation, even if what he did complied with regulations."

She'd begun to argue with him. He'd expected that. Still, that didn't make tonight any easier. "I was talking about saving lives, Kara. He was hung up on costs. Schedules."

When she blinked and kept her eyes closed longer than necessary he knew he'd hit a nerve. "Tell me something, Brand," she said. "If it had been you and someone had come to you, demanding to be heard, criticizing, would you have gone to your employers and told them you wanted to add to the project's cost—even though what you were doing already met seismic standards?"

"Damn it, Kara, it's not just that. There wasn't an earthquake and still the structure went down. Doesn't that tell you something?"

"Yes. Of course." She barely got the words out. "Why do you think I'm fighting for answers? Brand, please look at things from my perspective. You went to the authorities because my father wouldn't listen to what you were telling him about an additive no one requires. That doesn't make the building collapse his fault."

Didn't it? He was responsible for it. Where else had he cut costs? "Did he tell you what he said to me?"

"No."

No. "He didn't order me off the site. I suppose I ought to give him credit for that. What he did was get in my face and tell me he was sick of engineers, architects, and building officials putting constraints on him. Either they have faith in his ability to do a job, or they can get another man. That went double for me."

"Yes." She drew out the word until he realized she was saying it more for herself than him. "He'd say that."

"Because he's stubborn and bullheaded."

"No," she said, even though she'd called her father exactly that a few days ago. "Because he has a great deal of pride about his skill. He resents it when anyone questions it. Only—" He watched her knuckles around her wine glass turn white and wondered if she was in danger of shattering it. "Only, the garage he was responsible for collapsed."

"Yes." He reached out and drew the glass out of her hand. She didn't seem to notice.

"And I have to know why."

He waited until she'd blinked and was focusing on him again. He wondered if anyone had noticed that neither of them had started their meals. "There's a number of reasons, Kara. Substandard materials, the placement of supporting beams, the depth of the reinforcing bars."

"In other words, you told the investigators that you suspected him of—of . . ."

"Of doing something either unethical or unprofessional."

She drew away as far as she could, her eyes spearing him with anger. Then the anger faded, and he knew he'd said things she'd thought herself. "Not my father," she whispered. "He's always taken such pride in his work."

"Then what?"

"I don't know. Oh God, he won't tell me. And you

don't have any answer for me, either. Look . . ." She leaned over and picked up her fanny pack which she'd placed on the floor beside her. Rummaging around, she found a pen and piece of paper and placed them on the table. "Explain to me about the polymer. What, exactly, did you tell him about it?"

As she wrote, Brand reconstructed the conversation as thoroughly as he could. Then, although he didn't want to do it, he gave her a blow by blow of everything he'd said to those responsible for the investigation. Finally, he was finished. For several moments she sat staring at what she'd been writing. She stirred herself when the waitress removed their untouched salads and brought the main dish. He tore apart his small sourdough loaf, buttered both halves and handed her one. She took a bite, then looked again at the piece of paper.

"You called him a lot of things."

"I didn't call him anything. I simply said—"

"Don't play semantics with me, Brand. Whether you came in ranting like some avenger or coolly and logically outlined your concerns, the bottom line is that you raised some very serious questions about my father's ability to do his job."

He said nothing; there was nothing to say.

"You're saying you think he's one of three things: a cheat, a fool, or incompetent."

A few weeks ago those words wouldn't have fazed him. Yes, when you got past the polite phraseology, that's exactly what he'd said. Back then, because he'd been driven by the memory of Hank's fear and pain, the near tragedy, he hadn't cared. Now he'd met Hank's sister. Learned about the other side of Art Crayton. "That's not my decision to make. The investigators—"

"You're the one who went to them—started them questioning my—"

"Wait a minute. There'd be a probe whether I said anything or not."

"But—" She picked up her fork and speared something in her stew. "Everything wouldn't be focused on my dad if you hadn't gotten your hackles up over the way he treated you."

Was that right?

She stared at what was on her fork. "The collapse could have been caused by something entirely beyond his control. Did you ever think of that?"

He had, not when physical pain and fear and a horrible memory drove his words, but later when he'd had time to calm down. "We're arguing about something neither of us can resolve. When the investigation is completed, and the conclusions are made public—"

"But in the meantime my father can't work. He's probably not even going to be allowed to help with the clean-up. How do you think that makes him feel?"

Like someone who'd had the props knocked out from under him. But if Art turned out to be any of the things Kara had just accused him of saying—halfway through the thought, Brand stopped staring at her and focused on his own stew. Because there were only a few crumbs of bread left, he realized he must have finished that, but he hadn't touched the rest of the meal. He picked up his fork and, like Kara, jabbed into the middle of the large, steaming bowl. When he lifted his fork, he saw he'd speared a piece of meat.

"What are you going to do?" he asked and placed the meat in his mouth.

"Talk to my father, again." She indicated her notes. "And if he *still* won't talk to me, maybe I'll approach the investigators one more time."

"They won't tell you anything, not now."

She placed her fork on the side of her plate and slowly began folding the paper she'd been writing on. He noticed that her hand was trembling, and that she wasn't trying to hide the fact from him. He also took note of the way the lighting caught the moisture in her eyes. "It won't be much longer," he said softly. "Then you'll know. We'll all know."

Although she blinked several times, her eyes continued to look damp. He couldn't stop staring, couldn't tell himself that her tears were none of his business.

When she finally spoke, he heard the catch in her throat. "Yes. We will. And nothing will ever be the same between my father and me again."

EIGHT

Because they'd gone to the restaurant together, Kara had no option but to climb back into Brand's truck and sit beside him while he drove her home. She could think of nothing to say and was glad he respected her silence. When he started to turn off the engine, she told him not to bother and slid out of the cab. She thanked him for the meal and told him she'd see him at work. Then, without looking back at him, she walked away. Before she reached the cabin, she heard the truck take off.

For several minutes after stepping inside, she didn't bother to turn on any lights. Instead she kicked off her shoes and sank into the blanket-covered couch. Sighing, she slid down on her spine until she could rest her head on the back of the couch.

The evening's conversation swirled around her. Knowing Brand as she did, she understood why he'd approached her father about the polymer. And knowing her father, she knew why he hadn't greeted Brand's "suggestion" with open arms.

It was too late to call home. Even if she could get her thoughts together to present her father with Brand's version of things, she didn't want to risk keeping him awake tonight.

No. That wasn't all of it. She didn't want her father to know what she'd done, what she'd learned, what she thought. Not yet.

Not until she knew how to tell him that she'd had no choice.

Head aching, she pushed herself to her feet and walked over to the corner area that served as her bedroom. She turned on the lamp by her single bed and looked around at the newly repaired and painted plaster walls, taking comfort from her surroundings. She'd rescued an old quilt from Ada's storage closet and washed it. Now the slightly ragged but well-crafted quilt covered her bed. The bold mix of colors brightened the room. That, plus the fact that she'd left a window open and the clean scent of pine and mountain air filled the room, lifted her spirits slightly. No matter what happened now, at least she'd been honest with Brand. She no longer hid anything from him.

Except what she felt whenever he came near, whenever thoughts of him invaded her unguarded mind.

She removed her clothes and slipped into a robe before padding back out into what she referred to as her living room. Because she didn't want to be alone with her thoughts, she turned on the small stereo she'd bought from one of her co-workers and selected a country and western tape. Although the rhythm reminded her of when she'd danced with Brand, she couldn't bring herself to turn it off. Feeling both foolish and restless, she moved in a slow, sweeping circle in the middle of the room, her arms outstretched as if to encircle a partner.

She didn't have to be with him to remember what his deep voice sounded like. Her arms remembered how it felt to be around his powerful body. She easily called up the spiced scent of his aftershave, the way his thick, dark hair slid over his forehead, the equally dark eyes reaching beneath her surface to deep, unprotected layers.

She imagined that he'd pulled her closer and was whispering something to her—maybe inviting her to spend Sunday with him. They'd be new with each other. There'd be nothing between them except the exploration of a budding, promising relationship. Her father wouldn't—

Out of the corner of her eye she glimpsed something pass by her front window. A second later she heard a knock at the door, and embarrassed, dropped her arms and walked over to let Ada in. Although it was barely nine o'clock, Ada had changed into night clothes, too. She held up a box decorated with gaudy glass beads and faded red velvet. "I found it, finally." She planted the box on the coffee table before turning to face Kara. "The antique jewelry I told you about that I got when my aunt died."

A few days ago when Kara told her the story behind her cameo necklace, Ada had explained that she'd been given some costume jewelry as part of her aunt's estate, and although she wouldn't be seen dead in most of it, she'd hung onto the pieces. Kara had expressed interest in seeing the collection.

Only, with her mind on everything she and Brand had said to each other, she wasn't sure she was up to a conversation about earrings and bracelets. But before she could think how to suggest that another time might be better, Ada had upended the box on the coffee table and was rummaging through the pile she'd created, obviously eager to talk. "I saw Brand drive off a few minutes ago," she said. "When I saw you two pull up, I thought he might stay a while. All right, I hoped he'd stick around. That's one sexy man, not that I should have to tell you that. But he must have a lot to do getting ready for tomorrow and all."

"He must." Kara started to separate one long necklace from another, glad to have something to do. "You've really had all this in a box? Maybe your aunt wanted it treated with a little more respect.''

Ada held aloft a choker necklace made from bright red beads. She tried to place it around her thick neck, then winced as the beads cut into her flesh. ''I'm not the jewelry type. You know that. You'd think the rest of the family would have given me something I'd have more use for. I didn't want much, just a little reminder of one of the world's last grand old dames.'' She dropped the choker and picked up a single ''pearl'' earring so large that it nearly covered her ear. ''I can't believe anyone would really wear this stuff. Anyone except my aunt, that is. She really was a character. Do you have any aunts?''

Kara explained that her father had been an only child and her mother had two unmarried brothers. Her attention was drawn to a ring made from a piece of onyx so dark that almost no light reflected from its depths. Brand's eyes had been like that much of tonight, dark and secretive. She started to pick up the ring, then withdrew her hand. Idly, she ran her fingers over several other pieces. Ada was saying something about her aunt, but she couldn't make herself concentrate on the words. Brand had two parents, and a clean, uncomplicated relationship with them. Until a few weeks ago, she believed the same about her and her father.

''Kara, what's the matter?''

''The matter? Nothing.''

''Don't give me that.'' Ada leaned forward and brought her face so close to Kara's that her features started to blur. ''I was telling you about the time my aunt insisted on riding a zoo elephant even though she was nine months pregnant. I'm sure you didn't hear a word.''

Elephant? Pregnant? ''I'm sorry. I guess my mind was wandering.''

''Toward Brand?''

If Kara thought she could keep anything from Ada tonight, she was fast learning how wrong she was. For a moment she debated telling her anything, then decided she needed someone to talk to. She wanted to keep her story brief, but she knew she'd been talking for almost ten minutes before she came to the end.

"Oh honey, it's really gotten complicated, hasn't it?"

"It wouldn't be if my father had been upfront with me. But I understand how hard this is for him. His pride—"

"Pride's only part of it. Men!" Ada patted her hand. "Them and their damn egos."

Kara almost laughed. She would have if things hadn't been so serious. "If they conclude he's responsible for the collapse, he isn't going to have much of an ego left."

"I know. I know." While she was talking, Ada had eased herself closer on the couch. Now she was sitting only a few inches away, looking for all the world like a worried mother hen. "But right now you can't do anything about how this is affecting your father, can you?"

"No."

"That's right. The only emotions you can deal with are your own. Tell me, what bothers you the most about all of this?"

Because she sensed true concern behind Ada's question, Kara searched her heart and mind for the answer. There, half hidden by everything that had been swirling through her, was a single, clean thought. She didn't know how to deal with how she felt about Brand Lockwood. Still, when she spoke, she kept that to herself. "I guess I'm afraid my relationship with my father will never be the same."

"Why? Because he might be convicted of something?"

Convicted! The word sliced through her. "No." She shook her head. "Whether he's guilty or innocent, he's still my father."

"That he might never be able build again and that the balance in your family will change."

"That's part of it."

"But not much."

What was Ada getting at? "No. Not really. If he has to leave construction, he'll find a way to support himself. That's the kind of man my father is." She concentrated on the wall opposite her. Despite two coats of paint, the uneven wallboard showed. Maybe paneling. Panel? In a few months, she'd no longer be here. "It's just that I'm afraid nothing else will satisfy him the way building does. I can't see him putting his heart and soul into any other career."

"Then you're afraid he'll lose some of his zest for life?"

"He already has," she admitted. "This has been an incredible blow for him."

"But it doesn't change the way you feel about him, does it?"

She shook her head, waiting for Ada to explain herself. Without saying a word, Ada took her hand, leathered old flesh against what was both firm and smooth. "What I'm asking is, will you stop loving your father?"

Kara couldn't keep her eyes open. The question pulled her into herself, down into that quiet place where emotions lived. Surrounded by them and Ada's concern, she continued. "He's my father. I wouldn't be who I am without him. What I feel for him will never change."

"I knew it. And you know he feels the same way. Honey, tell him everything you've told me. That's what he needs to hear. Everything else comes after that."

For a moment Kara locked herself around the words. Then, as Ada's wisdom seeped into her, she opened her eyes and gave the older woman a grateful smile. She blinked back tears. "You're right," she whispered.

"I know I am." Ada released Kara and rubbed her hands together in a self-satisfied gesture. "That's what I keep telling that old fool I married, that I'm always right. Haven't quite convinced him yet, but I'm wearing him down.'' Then, features once again grave, she leaned closer. ''Kara, I have another question. One that might not be as easy to answer.''

None of the questions she'd been grappling with since the accident were easy. She couldn't imagine which one had come to the forefront of Ada's mind.

''I'm a nosy, interfering old lady who's going to pose something to you. I know you don't want to hear it even less than I want to be saying it. But it's something I'm sure you've already thought about, at least on a subconscious level. I'm thinking you need to get it out in the open.''

''What?''

''What—'' Ada sighed. ''What if it turns out that Brand was right in going to this committee, or whatever you call it, about his concerns regarding your father's competence? If Brand's testimony leads to a conviction, if you find out that your father's negligence, or whatever, jeopardized your brother's life, how will that change the way you feel about Brand?''

''Brand?'' She blinked. ''This is about my father.''

''Is it?''

Had Ada seen through her carefully casual words about Brand's role in all this? Had Ada heard emotion that she herself could only guess at? After everything she'd already shared with Ada, she couldn't shy away now—any more than she could shy away from herself. ''I don't know how I feel about him at this moment,'' she admitted. ''How can I say what might happen in a few days?''

To her surprise, Ada started shaking her head. ''It's happening, isn't it?''

''What's happening?''

''Can't you see it? No. I don't suppose you can, not with everything else you've had to deal with. Kara, Kara—'' Ada picked up her hand again and began rubbing it briskly. ''You're falling in love with him.''

* * *

No. She's wrong, Kara told herself repeatedly as she got ready for work the next morning. Okay, so she was attracted to Brand—she wasn't going to try to deny that. But love? She'd been in love before, at least she thought she'd loved Scott. With him . . . She yanked on her boots and swallowed the last of her coffee. Try as she might, she couldn't remember what about her former husband had attracted her to him.

She couldn't get her mind to stay on Scott at all.

"Well, I'm not," she told Mooch as she stepped outside. "I'd have to be an absolute fool to let that happen." As if *let* had anything to do with falling in love, she wondered as she knocked on her landlord's front door. As she waited, she stared at the weathered porch boards that creaked every time she stepped onto them. She'd fix them when she got home. Ada had told her not to bother, but plunging into a repair job tonight would give her something to do.

Ada, already dressed, opened the door. The tantalizing aroma of cinnamon filled the air. Kara was afraid Ada had deliberately gotten up early because she'd asked if she could call her father before going to work. Ada assured her that wasn't the case at all. "You know we don't mind if you come in any time you need to use the phone. I'm rattling around baking something I shouldn't eat because I didn't sleep that well last night. That happens sometimes when you get to be my age."

It happens at any age, Kara admitted, thinking of her own restless night. Although she could sense Ada watching her and knew the older woman would like nothing better than to take up last night's conversation all over again, she hinted that she was willing to offer her services as cinnamon roll tester, then went to the phone and dialed. Her brother sounded wide awake, but when she got her father on the line, his voice was sleep-slowed.

"I wanted to reach you before I went to work," she explained. Leaning against a wall for support, she stared at Ada without really seeing the woman. "Dad, Brand knows who I am."

"What?" Her father fairly snorted the word. "I thought you gave me your word you wouldn't say anything."

Because she'd already steeled herself for that reaction from her father, she was able to weather it. "It wasn't a matter of 'give.' You tried to force me. Besides, I didn't have a choice. I couldn't be around him every day and continue to be dishonest with him. Eventually he would have found out. Dad, don't you understand? It would have only made things worse if he'd heard it from someone else."

For the better part of a minute, her father didn't say anything. Finally, he cleared his throat. "How'd he take it?"

"How did he take learning who I am? He was surprised, shocked."

"Shocked? He really hates me that much, does he?"

That wasn't it at all. Brand's reaction, she sensed, had been wrapped up in a lot of things—like a dance, a kiss, a walk along a windswept dock. Because she didn't want to tell her father about those things, she simply told him that she and Brand had spent several hours together last night. She now knew what Brand had said to the investigators, as well as his side of the discussion he and Art had had. "He said you weren't very receptive to the innovations he tried to suggest."

"Did he tell you he practically rammed them down my throat?"

Because he was driven by the memory of what happened to him at nineteen. While she'd been talking, Ada had gone into the kitchen. Now she returned with two cups of hot chocolate and handed one to Kara. She took a tentative sip before telling her father that she found the possibilities for the new polymer fascinating. "Are you sure you wouldn't have been able to talk the owners into going for the added expense? When I think of the long-term bene-fits—"

"I didn't have time, Kara. You know what it's like to be under a deadline. The polymer isn't required. I wasn't breaking any regulation. What is it, are you questioning me, too? Brand's gotten to you?"

Gotten to me? Maybe. Yes, Dad, maybe. Quickly she explained that she wasn't going to take sides. All she wanted was the truth, at least enough to help the Crayton family prepare for the findings.

"So you took notes, did you?" her father cut in before she was done. "Are you going to send them to me or keep me guessing?"

This wasn't like her father. He'd never in his life gone looking for an argument with her. Had she hurt him that much? And then maybe his reaction was simply an accu-mulation of too much stress. "I'll send you everything I have, Dad. I'd be happy to, you know that. But I'm not sure what good it'll do us right now. Until—"

"I could have told you that. Why do you think I didn't want you talking to the man? All you did was waste your breath trying to ram your way into something I wanted to handle myself. I always thought you were smarter than this."

No. This wasn't the father she knew. She locked eyes with Ada, but of course the other woman couldn't tell her anything. "Dad, I didn't call you to start a fight. I just wanted to be honest with you."

"Honest?"

What was that note in her father's voice? "You sound tired," she said, trying to take the conversation in a less dangerous direction.

"I guess I am, not that I'm probably saying something

you haven't already heard from your brother. Honey, what . . ."

"Honey, what?" she prompted when his voice trailed off.

"Nothing. You're doing all right? The job's not too hard?"

"I can do the job in my sleep. The country's magnificient. The sense of history is everywhere. I know you'd like it. Dad, I'm getting paid this Friday. I'll send the money right away."

He didn't say anything, and she understood that his pride had gotten in the way of words. She was sorry she'd had to put it to him like that, but she didn't know how to sidestep the truth. "It's a hard time for all of us," she said, taking comfort from Ada's concerned look. "It's bound to put a strain on our relationship. But certain things never change. Like how much I love you."

"Love? Oh honey, you don't know how much I needed to hear that."

His admission scared her. She'd always known she was loved; he should have, too. The fabric of their relationship ran rich and deep, and usually unsaid. "You doubted it?" she had to ask.

"I'm doubting a lot of things these days."

There. Finally they were getting close to the core of things. Although it was time for her to leave for work, she couldn't make herself rush the conversation. "I wish I could make that different for you."

"You can't. No one can. Kara? Do you know what was the worst for me? Not seeing the garage going down, although I'll never forget what that looked and sounded like. Not even knowing it was all on my shoulders. But when I first saw your brother . . ."

Oh God. "I know, Dad, I know." She couldn't get her voice above a whisper and could only hope that he'd be able to hear her.

"I've always done my best. Always tried to be good at what I do. I take pride—you know that. Honey?"

She said nothing, knowing he would talk when he was ready.

"Honey, you talked about those polymers. That's not the only thing Lockwood brought up. New technology, he's up on all of that. He—he talked about products and innovations I've never heard of."

Oh Dad.

"Maybe I haven't been keeping up. Maybe—that's what been so damn hard about all this. Questioning myself."

Her father had never in his life opened himself up to her like that. She found herself shaking and took a deep swallow of hot chocolate, hoping it would help. "Dad?" She barely got the word out and tried again. "Dad? When you get the money from me, if you can possibly swing it, why don't you and Hank buy air tickets and fly up here. I'd love to see you."

"You'd have time to spend with us?"

"I'll make time. You know that."

"That—that's good to hear. Honey, the results—I don't know when they'll be out."

"I understand. You don't feel you can be gone long. But please think about it," she pressed. "That's all I ask. Think about it."

When her father repeated that he'd have to mull over her offer some more and weigh it against his responsibilities, she reluctantly told him she had to go to work and promised him she'd write him this evening. Finally, although it was the last thing she wanted to do, she put an end to the conversation. She replaced the receiver, then stood looking at her hand, eyes feeling hot and dry. She couldn't think how to make herself move until she felt Ada pull the warm cup out of her hand. "I hate seeing you go through this," Ada said.

"I hate going through it." She gave Ada a shaky smile. "I love that old cuss. I think he gave me more of himself this morning than he has in a long time. Not all I need, but enough for a start. Anything, just so he isn't bottling it all up inside him."

"You did the right thing. He might not have wanted his daughter, his little girl, pushing him, but you got him to open up. Like you said, it's a beginning."

"I hope. He has to have someone to talk to, and maybe Hank and I are the only ones."

When Ada hugged her around the waist, for a moment Kara couldn't do anything except hug back. "Thank you," she whispered. "I'm sure, when you rented the cabin to me, you never thought you'd have a tenant crying on your shoulder."

Ada gently pushed her away and held her firmly at arms' length. "You listen to me, young lady. I'll get a crying towel for my shoulder if things get too soggy. Believe me, I don't mind at all being here for you to talk to. But—" She gave Kara's arms a quick squeeze. "I'm not the one you should be going to. You know that."

Brand's truck was already parked in its usual place when Kara got to work, but she didn't see him with any of the crew members. After getting her assignment from Chuck, she started her bulldozer and drove it a half mile further up the mountain to where work was being done on widening a sharp switchback. It was another typical summer Alaska morning—sunny one minute, cloudy the next. Because the temperature remained fairly constant in the cab, she was able to watch the changing sky-scape without being too affected by it.

Except emotionally, she admitted as snatches of conversation both from last night and this morning continued to play and replay in her mind.

After a couple of hours of piling up crushed rock and

tamping it down, she stopped so the backed-up cars and buses could thin out. As she sat listening to her machine's smooth idling, she sensed that she was being watched. Discounting quick glances from the passing tourists, she looked around. After a moment she spotted Brand. From what she could tell, he'd been talking to Stella, but since the Indian woman was putting her hardhat back on, apparently their conversation was finished.

She didn't consider the day that warm, but Brand had removed his shirt. The dappled sunlight coming through the evergreens painted his chest in dancing shades of light and dark. Sweat glistened on him, answering her question. He'd been doing something strenuous and had removed his shirt in order to cool off.

He was also looking at her, his eyes so deep in shadow that she couldn't read his mood. Not that she was interested in mood. As long as his jeans rode low on his narrow hips and her fingers ached to press themselves against the hard ridge of his collarbone, she couldn't think of anything except what he was physically.

Physical. The word ran through her, absorbing her.

She couldn't say how long he simply watched her before leaving Stella and walking over to her. She couldn't take her mind and eyes off his progress, couldn't wrench herself free of his physical impact. She saw the way each step twisted him slightly at the waist, how his arms moved slowly, sensually at his side. And for too long she forgot to breathe.

"You're all right?" he asked when he was close enough that they could carry on a conversation. From where she sat in the high cab, she now looked down on the breadth of his shoulders, thought about that strength surrounding her.

"All right?" At the last instant, she stopped herself from licking her lips.

"After last night? You were able to sleep?"

You know better than that; you must. "Some," she said with what honesty she dared. She studied the taut line of his neck as he looked up at her. Now she could see into his eyes and knew that his entire attention was riveted on her. "I talked to my father this morning."

"I thought you might. How is he?"

Not, how did he react to what you told him, but how is he. "Tired. He sounded old."

"Did he?"

Brand was waiting for her to tell him more, to reveal other facets of her father. That was none of Brand's business and yet . . . and yet at this moment she wanted to make love to him and short of that wanted to trust him enough to reveal more of her father's vulnerability.

Only her father's vulnerability.

"I invited him to come up here."

"Why?"

Couldn't Brand guess? In a voice she had to fight to retain control over, she explained that, if anything, she was even more worried about her father's health than she had been before and needed to see him, talk to him, nag him to take care of himself. "He hasn't committed himself to coming. With the way everything's hanging fire—"

"I wouldn't think he'd want to get this close to me."

If he does, I'll protect him from you. I'll . . . Brand had turned slightly so that the sun was no longer in his eyes. The movement caused him to spread his legs so he could straddle a small rock pile. His arms still hung by his side. His bulk, the hardened muscles of his chest, forced his arms slightly away from his body. He looked ready—for what? Action, yes. But what kind of action? Maybe he was readying himself for the moment when he'd have her in his arms.

What was she thinking?

Brand had asked her a question. She had to ask him to

repeat it. He wanted to know whether her family might arrive this weekend.

"No. They—they wouldn't have the money by then."

"I see."

Of course you do. For a moment her angry reaction surprised her, but then she understood. Being near Brand had her off balance; everything she felt was out of sync. Not sure what, if anything, she was supposed to say, she ran her hands over the gears, feeling their strength. Thinking of another kind of strength.

"Kara?"

She focused on him.

"I did something first thing this morning. I have two tickets for a ride on the narrow-gauge railroad."

Two tickets. Strangely, his gesture calmed her. "Do you?" she said.

"For this Sunday. I'd like you to go with me."

Her grip around the lever tightened. "Even now, knowing who I am?"

"Because I know who you are. Kara, look, I've been telling myself that what's happened doesn't have to result in a chasm between you and me. We've been pretty honest with each other lately. I want that kind of honesty to continue."

She stared down at him, trying to draw what he was thinking and feeling out of him and into her. She wanted to believe what she thought she saw. She wasn't sure she dared. "If my father's indicted, we're going to be at opposite ends of things."

"I know that. I also know that when Cliff and Ada told us about what this area has to offer, the richness of its history, we reacted the same way. It's something we both want to learn more about."

She wanted to buy his explanation, wanted to tell herself that they'd simply do some exploration together. But the sweat on his flesh hadn't dried and he'd just taken a deep, chest-expanding breath. She felt herself turn hot and hungry. "I don't know."

"Are you afraid of me?"

I'm afraid of me. "No. Of course not."

"Then what?"

Surely he knew the answer to that. But if he didn't, she wasn't going to tell him. "All right." She pushed the words out of her. "Sunday. The narrow-gauge."

"And, soon, the museum. And before the summer's over, I want to hike the Chilkoot with you."

"Do you?"

"That and more. Kara, I want to explore what's happening between us. I believe it's something we need to do."

NINE

When Brand held up a finely detailed scrimshaw carving of a magnificent gray wolf, Kara nodded approval. "Oh yes. I'm sure she'll love it."

Brand's sigh would have made a Shakespearean tragedy actor proud. "I hope so. It is *so* hard coming up with something for my mother. Like she says, at her age she's either already cluttered her house with it or she doesn't want it."

"But this represents a piece of the world you're living in these days," Kara said as the saleswoman in the little gift shop began wrapping Brand's purchase. "Don't forget, it's the thought you're after here."

"I hope you're right." Brand rested his head on the top of hers and sighed deeply as if the effort of buying his mother a birthday present had exhausted him. "I suppose I'm going to have to give you a finder's fee for what you've done."

Drawing away from him a little, Kara did her best to bat her lashes at him. Unfortunately, she'd never taken eyelash batting in school and wound up feeling as if she had a tic. "You dragged me past that ice cream stand in

159

your rush to get here. Wouldn't even let me check out their flavors. I'll tell you what; indulge me in a double scoop and we'll call it even."

Brand shook his head and sighed again, this time for the clerk's benefit. "The past few evenings have been impossible on my pocketbook. What do you have for a stomach, a bottomless pit?"

Last night Brand had grabbed a couple of deli sandwiches from a cafe down the street so they'd have something to eat before taking in the Trail of '98 Museum with its vivid photographic history of an era rugged beyond belief. She was glad he'd thought to buy dinner first since they'd wound up staying in the museum until it closed. True, Brand had been the one finally to haul her away from the park ranger who'd been patiently answering her questions about early day communication—what there was of it—but she hadn't let him forget that he'd insisted on watching the film three times.

"What bottomless pit?" she shot back. "You're the one who groused about having pizza withdrawal. If I recall, it was nine o'clock at night when you insisted on trying to find one. And going for eleven when you finished eating."

Shrugging, Brand dismissed her comment. "There's never a bad time for pizza. All right, bottomless pit, ice cream it is."

When they left the gift shop, now arguing over whether licorice-flavored ice cream was fit for human consumption, Kara knew they looked like a perfectly normal couple with nothing more on their minds than enjoying an evening together.

The incredible thing was she truly had enjoyed the past few evenings with Brand. Their conversations had never gotten more serious than what to buy his mother for her birthday, but she wanted it that way and suspected he did, too. Despite the sense of unease she felt around him— when he stood too close to her, when his eyes took on those dark hues she knew all too well, when her hands ached with the need to touch him—she'd rather be with him than apart.

At least, during all those off work hours, he hadn't taken her in his arms or tempted her with his lips. And although she sometimes sensed a battle going on within him, too, she did nothing to test the boundaries of their unspoken relationship.

The ice cream shop was little more than walk-in closet size and had only a dozen flavors to choose from. In addition, there was a large display of rock candy, gaudy earrings, and postcards, a mix she didn't pretend to understand. Kara chose something called rocky road mint and informed Brand that he had no imagination when he selected strawberry.

She was already back outside enjoying the endless evening light when she realized Brand hadn't followed her. Because another couple had entered the store, she remained where she was, watching a small buckboard drawn by two black horses take a load of tourists down the street. She waved at a couple of young boys sitting next to the sleepy-looking driver. The boys gave her a smile and wave in return, then she turned her thoughts to how quiet and peaceful Skagway looked with the surrounding mountains to protect it and keep it separate from the rest of the world.

Last night she and Brand had met a member of the city council who was also part of the volunteer fire department. According to him, Skagway was no different from any other town, except that it had never tried to separate itself from its past. He was right. If she ignored such things as cars and telephone poles, she could easily imagine herself as a gold-hungry miner.

Maybe not. The idea of slogging through miles and mountains of snow didn't appeal to her. She could be a dance hall girl, flirting with grimy customers, wearing a dress that probably wouldn't survive another washing, spending her nights . . . okay, not a dance hall girl. What did that leave? She could run a mercantile; the thought bored her to death.

That's what was wrong with researching history. The rose-colored glasses came off.

When she'd finished her cone and Brand still hadn't emerged, she turned back around, thinking to tease him about being slow. Just then, he stepped out of the little shop, a small paper bag tucked suspiciously under his arm. When she cocked her head, indicating it, he informed her that its contents were none of her business, at least not until he'd decided she'd done something to earn its contents.

"Fine," she informed him. "I hope you bought enough of that hard candy to rot out all your teeth. It'd serve you right to have to eat it all yourself. Now, if we're going to be boarding the—what's it called?—White Pass something train bright and early tomorrow morning, I suggest you take me home."

"You don't want to do any more shopping? There's an antique store—"

"No more shopping, please!" She pointed at her feet. "My boss, a real slave driver, kept me on the run all day. My dogs are aching."

"They wouldn't be if you were in any kind of shape."

She knew he'd intended it as a casual comment. She tried to take it as such. But he stood a few inches away on the weathered wooden sidewalk dressed in a red flannel shirt that made him look incredibly rugged and potent, somehow timeless. He would have been one of the few to survive a winter of mining deep in the wilderness. If he came into her dance hall, she wouldn't send him packing.

To assure herself that she'd keep her hands off him, she tucked them in her back pockets, but she couldn't remember how to break eye contact. He'd been smiling, looking like a boy contemplating a long, choreless weekend. Now, slowly, gracefully, his mouth went soft. Soft. Her mind swirled around the word and the promise that went with it. She fought to keep from licking her lips, won the battle, but couldn't think of a thing to say.

Was he having the same problem? With his eyes becoming darker by the minute, she thought so.

No. They couldn't pretend to be anything except casual friends.

Unable to break free of whatever it was he'd wrapped around her, she slid a couple of inches closer and tilted her head upward. A small, desperate voice screamed at her to stop; she couldn't hold onto the reason. She felt so weak that she wasn't sure she could go on standing, and yet as long as he stood there, looking down at her with his incredibly dark and beautiful eyes, she would match him strength for strength, challenge for challenge.

The buckboard rattled down a side street, distracting her only a little. The other couple left the ice cream shop and a man with two children in tow passed behind Brand. Brand went on looking at her; she remained in his spell.

Then, out of the corner of her eye, she caught a glimpse of something sweeping through the sky above him. When the movement was repeated, she realized she'd spotted an eagle. It seemed right; Brand should be backdropped by one of Alaska's great wild creatures.

"What are you looking at?"

Had she really pulled her attention away from him? She must have; when she focused on him again, the silent challenge was gone from his eyes and she could think again. Almost. Shaken, feeling lost somehow, she told him about the eagle. Her voice started small and weak but soon took on strength.

"I'm sorry I didn't see it," he told her. Then, before the silence that stretched on after his words could become awkward, he handed her his package. She took the crumpled bag with fingers that seemed overheated at the tips and, still meeting his gaze, opened it. Finally, she reached in and pulled out a pair of earrings in the shape of eagles in flight. If they'd been carved from ivory or fashioned from gold, they might have had some redeeming value, but they were plastic, bright red, with some kind of purple beads for eyes and talons that looked as if rigor mortis had set in. The eagles' beaks were filled with oversized silver and red fish. The fish's mouths gaped open and their red eyes bulged.

"What is this?"

"My gift to you. I saw you admiring them."

"I don't know what you saw, but it wasn't admiration. Please tell me I don't have to wear them."

Brand looked crestfallen. "I can't take them back. The clerk said the sale was final."

"No wonder. She was afraid she'd never find another sucker."

Still looking crushed, Brand took one of the earrings from her and held it near her ear. He then smiled and cocked his head, giving the effect serious consideration. "The color matches your eyes."

"My eyes are *not* red."

"Close enough." He draped a heavy arm over her shoulder, still grinning. "How's this? I'll take you home so you can get that beauty sleep you so desperately need. However, when I pick you up tomorrow, I expect you to show proper appreciation for my gift."

Kara drew in air, preparing to let out a long-suffering breath, but he'd kept his arm around her shoulder and when she looked up at him, she remembered how he'd looked standing there, waiting for her, when the eagle distracted her.

It was going to happen again. Tomorrow or the next day she'd look at him, be drawn into him and hear the hungry beating of her heart. The next time there might not be an eagle.

* * *

At least a half dozen times before Brand arrived to take her to the train station, Kara tried to come up with the words to tell him she couldn't go with him after all. That the tentative peace they'd established in the past few evenings was too fragile to hold during an entire day together.

But if she did that, he wouldn't see her in her new earrings and she'd always wonder what the day would have been like.

For one of the few times in her life she'd had trouble deciding what to wear. Finally she'd chosen a deep green chambray shirt with long sleeves she could roll up in case the temperature fluctuated. Usually she wore the shirttail out, but this time she tucked it into her jeans. There was nothing wrong with a touch of femininity she told herself as she unbuttoned a shirt button, leaving a few more inches of flesh uncovered. Three seconds later she nearly changed her mind. She was a heavy equipment driver after all, not a seductress. Then, driven by a sense of anticipation and danger, she left things the way they were. Something *was* simmering beneath the surface between her and Brand. Hadn't she'd been aware of him as a man from the beginning? Pretending it was otherwise wouldn't change reality.

Besides . . . no. She wasn't going to address whatever that "besides" might be.

When Brand arrived, she was more than a little grateful for the distraction from her thoughts. Although they had a few minutes before they needed to leave for the first train ride of the day, she didn't invite him in. Instead, when she heard him pull up, she hurried outside, nearly tripping over Mooch. After giving the dog the attention he demanded, she opened the truck door and hoisted herself into the high cab.

When she looked at Brand, she had a casual, playful expression carefully in place. "See." She indicated her ears. "I'm wearing them. However, if they poke me in the neck one more time, they're history."

His attention remained on her earrings for nearly a second. Then, making her incredibly aware of what he was doing, he lowered his gaze. Without saying a word, he let her know that he'd taken note of the deep V in her shirt.

She didn't try to explain; she barely understood.

As they drove over to where they would board the train, Kara told him she'd talked to her father and brother after he dropped her off last night. From what they'd been able to find out, evidence on the collapse was still being collected, but there were growing rumors that clean-up would soon begin, indication that the on-site work was nearly complete. Brand nodded but said nothing. She dropped the subject, aware that this was the first time in days either of them had brought up what stood between them.

Although the streets of Skagway were still quiet, enough visitors were on hand at the station to fill the small, historic train. Kara sat next to the window with Brand pressed close beside her. To say the narrow wooden seats were comfortable would be a lie. However, with Brand so close, she seldom thought about anything except the warmth of his arm pressed against hers. Although she wanted to say something, anything, so her thoughts would have somewhere to go, for the first few minutes of the ride not a word entered her mind.

They were a pioneering couple, two brave adventurers who'd volunteered to ride the train on its maiden trip. Ahead lurked the possibility of avalanches, polar bears, outlaws.

But she didn't have to worry. Brand would take care of her.

Then they changed from the restored steam engine to diesel power and began to climb into the mountains. Because she'd seen short stretches of the track while working on the road, she hadn't expected to be so in awe of it. But the narrow-gauge had been hacked out of the mountains nearly a hundred years ago with nothing more than black powder and pry-bars. Thinking of that, she could only shake her head in disbelief and share that disbelief with Brand. Thirty men had lost their lives during construction, two when a 100-ton granite slab buried them. When they passed what the guide identified as the Mile High Line, Brand leaned against her and stared out. "I don't believe this." His tone echoed the amazement she felt. "Workmen had to be suspended by ropes here so they could do the necessary blasting. Incredible."

Kara followed the line of his pointing finger. "Incredible," she repeated. "What made them do it? That's what I don't understand. Why would a man, or woman, risk their lives like that?"

Settling back down, Brand slid his arm around her shoulder. He gripped her so tightly that she knew what was going through his mind. At least he'd never have to ask those in his employ to do something that dangerous.

From then on, Kara didn't try to keep emotional distance from Brand. He, too, seemed to have forgotten their unspoken agreement to be nothing except friends.

Another time and place, she would have been so tuned in to him that she wouldn't have known where she was. But as the awesome miles slowly passed under them, she became totally caught up in the rare experience, sharing it with Brand as if between them they had a single mind, a single heart.

At one point they passed over a canyon-spanning bridge that had once been the highest such structure in the world. Feeling as if she'd been suspended over the world, she gripped Brand's hand in silent wonder both of nature's grand plan and man's courage to build and conquer. A little further along, they looked out and down at what remained of the White Pass Trail and the bleached horse skeletons that stood as mute testimony to unbelievable hardships.

"We have it so easy," she whispered when she found her voice. "What our ancestors endured makes me incredibly grateful for what I have."

"Grateful, yes," Brand repeated. "But it's more than that. The fact that this railroad exists, and has for almost a hundred years, stuns me. Humbles me."

She wanted to tell Brand that this experience hadn't diminished her respect and admiration for his skills, but when she caught the continuing look of wonder in his eyes, she didn't. He was caught up in the past, in a rare and lasting experience.

And she was sharing it with him.

How long it took to climb to the international boundary between Alaska and Canada she couldn't say. As the engines were switched to the rear of the train for the ride back down the mountain, she stood on dirt and rock beside Brand, shivering a little because the wind blew free and uninhibited here. The day, which had begun as a mix of cloud and sun, had grown steadily darker. The sky turned gray, then began sliding into deep purple. "Maybe it's going to rain," Brand observed as they got back on the train. "Maybe enough that we won't be able to work tomorrow."

Maybe we'll spend the day together. For a moment the thought terrified her, then she stopped trying to deny what she wanted. With Brand sitting beside her again, she couldn't be anything except honest with herself. This man had no business in her life. In a few days what they'd shared could blow up around them. But this was today and his hard, warm body couldn't be ignored. "Maybe."

Just drop her off and get the hell out of there. For the third time since they left the train and hurried through drizzling rain to his truck, Brand tried to tell himself he wasn't going to step inside her cabin. But the world continued to be painted in cloaking shades of gray and deep purple. He felt everything closing down around them, pulling them closer and closer to each other. Separating them from everything else. She sat beside him, silent, watching people scurry along the wooden sidewalks. Despite her earlier threat, she continued to wear the gaudy earrings, but that wasn't what he noticed.

She hadn't dressed any differently from what he saw her in every day at work, and yet somehow it was different. Because she'd tucked in her shirt, he couldn't ignore her lean waist and the bold flair of her hips and her long, competent-looking legs. There was no way she couldn't be aware of what her blouse revealed. Had she done that to tease him? To test herself?

"It smells incredible." Her voice, small and gentle, echoed in the rapidly fogging cab. "There's something about the smell of rain that I don't think I'll ever get tired of."

"It smells wet."

She shot him a disgusted look. He waited for her to match his flippant comment. Instead, her eyes gentled, and she parted her lips slightly. He absorbed the gesture and tucked it safely into a quiet place deep inside him. If their exploration of each other ended abruptly, as he feared, he would always have the memory of her looking at him simply and honestly—wanting him.

She wanted him. He wondered if she knew that, then decided it didn't matter because if she wasn't now aware of her emotion, she would be before the day was over.

Drop her off. Get away, now. Before it's too late.

It already was.

He put his mind to the quick thunk of his truck tires as he drove over the bridge he'd helped build for Cliff and Ada. Then he was on packed earth again and that quieter sound hummed through him and freed him from the world beyond this time and place. Kara sat on her side of the truck, looking small and fragile in the three-quarter-ton vehicle. Today her hands weren't at the controls of a monster-sized piece of machinery. Instead, she'd rested them on her thighs, the ring her mother had given her a thin shadow on her sun-darkened flesh. He glanced at her throat even though he already knew she wore the slender cameo necklace. Those stupid earrings looking out of place—garish and cheap on a proud woman. A woman who'd given him a glimpse of velvet flesh beneath a practical shirt.

If she didn't invite him in, he'd respect her decision. But the truck cab had been invaded by an energy that had nothing to do with the growing storm. He pulled up as close to the cabin as he could and killed the motor. Looking over at her, he tapped the source of that energy. When he opened his door, she continued to stare out at the rain, now looking incredibly alive, potent, dangerous. He walked over to her side and yanked on the handle. She slid out, landing on the damp earth. For three, maybe four seconds, she met his eyes; he read emotions he could drown in.

Then, perhaps because she needed to take back control of herself, she looked up and let the rain drizzle down on her face and hair.

"Listen to that." Her voice reached out and encircled him. "The wind and rain in the trees. And the smell— oh, that smell."

Forget the rain. You're making me crazy. "It smells like pine," he said.

"No. It's more than that—more alive. Brand, ah—" He might be reading something into her that wasn't there, but he could have sworn he saw her give herself a shake. "Come on in, please."

What time was it? Mid-afternoon. Maybe she was planning to fix him something to eat since they hadn't had lunch, but he didn't give a damn about food. Watching the flow and roll of her hips, he followed her inside.

Somehow she'd found time to make more changes on the cabin, washing windows, removing the heavy old sheet curtains, wallpapering the wall closet to the kitchen area, giving the room a sense of space and freshness. He might have to go into the bathroom to find the source of the light aromas he'd learned were a part of her, but even standing in the living room with the rain tapping against the tin roof, he felt himself drowning in feminine scents.

"The roof isn't leaking," she whispered. "I can't believe it."

"Good. Good."

When she stood looking at him, her hair touched by liquid beads, he felt his body tighten with energy. Wanton? Wild? No. She was neither of those things. Every line of her body spoke of a basic competence, a proud, gentle intellect. Still, because the rain had locked them alone inside these walls, he could pretend.

He didn't know what to do with himself. He could ram his hands in his pockets, but he would still have to come up with something to say. Something to do.

Do. Acting on that half thought, he walked over to the kitchen area and opened her refrigerator. She had nothing but milk and orange juice to drink when he needed something much stronger. With her standing behind him now, he pulled out some leftover meatloaf and began cutting it up for sandwiches. Saying nothing, she handed him several pieces of bread and poured them each a glass of milk.

She said something about it being a good thing that the roof didn't leak because it would be next to impossible to repair in the rain, and he said something equally unnecessary about hoping Cliff and Ada didn't need to go out in the storm.

Only, the storm was in here, in him. Created by her.

They sat in the living room on opposite sides of the

couch, eating off paper plates while they watched the rain through her curtainless windows. He'd left on the light over the sink. Other than that, the cabin was lit only by the gray and purple day.

Slowly, in fits and starts, the rain grew in intensity. Now the roof gave off a powerful drumbeat of sound that filled the room. Filled him.

With half of his sandwich still uneaten, he got to his feet and stood over her. She looked up at him, looked deep into him. Said nothing. He sighted down the taut column of her throat, paused at the tiny cameo resting against her flesh, fastened finally at the smooth, creamy curves that hinted at full breasts.

"It's going to happen, Kara."

"Happen?"

"Unless I leave, now, it's going to happen. Do you want me to walk out the door?"

Although for a long time she said nothing, he knew he hadn't surprised her with his words. He read it in her eyes, in the fullness of her mouth, the unconscious way her body arched toward him. He'd placed *it* in front of them, honest and open. Now all he could do was wait for her response.

Finally: "No. Don't leave."

Don't leave. He almost asked her if she was sure of what she was doing, but he'd watched her make her decision. He thought he might have to help her to her feet; he wanted her so much that he had to fight to put off the contact. Instead, she placed her unfinished lunch on the battered old coffee table and rose gracefully to meet him. Not smiling, she covered his cheek with a warm hand. "I'm not very good at this sort of thing. Telling a man what's going on inside me."

"You don't have to tell me anything."

"Maybe. But I want to. I . . ." Her hand slid off him, whispered past his arm, rested by her side. "I don't want to talk about anything except here and now. Can you understand why? Honor it?"

He nodded. "Because that's the only way we're going to be able to make this work."

Although she winced a little at what he'd said, she nodded in return. "This is insane. I know better; I should know better. But Brand, if we don't explore certain things—if I try to lie to myself, and you, about what I want and need—I'll spend the rest of my life regretting it." She laughed a little, a sad kind of sound. "I'm going to regret it either way. That's the hell of it."

She was so brave and bold that her courage rocked him. "Not regret, Kara," he said, although, of course, he couldn't promise her that. "We might never get back what we have right now, but to say you'll regret today puts a lie to everything good that's happened between us."

Her lids slid slowly over her eyes and stayed that way for several long seconds. Then she lifted her lashes and smiled. This time the gesture carried a sense of strength with it. "Thank you for saying that. You're wise, so—"

"Not wise. Not wise at all."

When she cocked her head slightly to the side, he waited her out. He could tell her that when it came to what happened between a man and a woman—between them—he could only take one stumbling step after another. But surely she knew that.

For the second time, she covered his cheek with her hand. He felt the brush strokes of her fingers, waited while her warmth blended with his. He wondered if he would ever forget what it felt like to have her touch him like this. Then, before he could search inside himself for the answer, he blanketed her hand with his. Her eyes, riveted to his, spoke of fear and need. He cupped her hand and brought it around to his mouth where he painted it with tiny kisses. The fear went out of her.

Although his body already pulsed with the need to possess her, he fought to match her pace. Surely she'd want their lovemaking to be spun out one inch, one touch at a time.

Feeling as if he'd been absorbed by a power beyond his control, he bracketed her face, holding her there for him. He wanted to make that first kiss gentle, reverent, but power pulsed through him. When he felt her lips on his, he gave in to energy and crushed her against him. A little sound, half sigh, half cry, escaped her throat. He ignored it, listened instead only to what drove him.

Rain pounding on the roof. Blood pounding through his veins. And need—need beyond any he'd ever felt for a woman. She deserved to know what he felt.

With tongue and arms and fingers he explored her. Although her breath came quick and shallow when he pressed past her teeth and invaded her, she didn't draw away. Her fingers clutched his arms with such strength that he wondered, briefly, if she might leave bruises. Somehow he managed to keep from giving back in kind. Although she pressed herself against him, leg against leg, heavy breasts flattened against his chest, he never forgot that beneath jeans and heavy shirt was little more than a hundred pounds of life.

Wondering at the magic of her, of them, he drew back slightly. Through eyes that refused to focus, he stared at this woman who'd come into his life and taught him something new and wonderful and unnerving about who and what he was. He wanted to tell her that, to lay himself open to her.

But she drew her hands off his arms and pressed them against the base of his throat, first maybe to touch the pulse there. Then because she wanted to remove his shirt.

He stood, as restless as any teenage boy, watching. Waiting.

When she first felt the beat of Brand's heart beneath her fingers, Kara had to brace her legs to keep from swaying.

Miraculously her fingers were steady as, one by one, she pulled his buttons free and spread his shirt so that his chest was exposed and ready for her.

Ready.

The man was supposed to take the lead in such things, wasn't he? Women showed restraint and control. But her body had been absorbing the sound of rain on the roof for too long. She felt consumed by the hard-driving rhythm.

Still, they had the rest of this day. And the night. But when he stood, not moving, waiting, she drew the shirttail out of his waistband, slid the cotton fabric off his shoulders and dropped the garment onto the couch. Behind him, she could see the window with its shadowed view of a forest cloaked in rain. No one could reach them, touch them here. Cliff and Ada had to know Brand was with her, but they would leave them alone. And although Ada's eyes might later ask questions, her landlady and friend wouldn't say anything.

Only she and Brand would ever know what happened here.

Her attention shifted from the window back to him as if he'd commanded her. When she touched his naked chest, she did it with sensitized fingertips and palms. There, inches from her, lay his heart, beating. Always beating.

She could hear him breathing. The sound carried no rhythm as if he had lost control over its tempo. Wondering at her ability to do that to him, she ran her fingertips lightly over his nipples and down to the hard columns of his ribs. Inch by inch she crept lower, touched the waistband of his jeans, wrapped her fingers over the button that held it in place. For a moment the fabric resisted her effort, then it gave, sliding the zipper down a few inches. She reached for the metal tab, thinking—thinking what?

"No. Not yet."

His voice, so much like the throb of rain on a metal

roof, stopped her. She tried to meet his eyes, faltered, shook herself, succeeded this time.

"Why not?"

"Because it's my turn."

My turn. Made weak by two simple words, she rocked back on her heels, let her hands drop to her side, and waited. She might look in control of her emotions, but she felt as if she was being wrenched apart. In a minute, a second maybe, she'd lose what little of herself was left.

But until that moment came, she'd stand before him and let him do what he wanted with her.

He began with her earrings. She turned her head slightly so that he could see what needed to be done. Gently, teasing her senses with the effort, he drew the loops out of the tiny holes in her ears and let the plastic eagles drop to the couch on top of his shirt. His attention next went to her necklace, but although he ran his fingers over it several times, he left it on her.

His rough and hardened fingertips on her throat made her shudder. He smiled slightly, the look of a man who knew exactly what he was doing. But when he began working on her buttons, his movements were unsure, as if something had made him clumsy. Maybe the reason was no more complicated than what had happened to her because they were alone together.

A pulling at her waist brought her thoughts back from wherever they'd drifted. Somehow he'd unbuttoned her blouse without touching her. Now he freed her from the garment. It, too, landed on the couch, covering the gaudy earrings. She wore a front-fastening sports bra, practical, laceless. Still barely bringing his fingers in contact with her, he flicked the snap free and drew the straps first off one shoulder and then the other.

When he extended his hands—oh, so slowly—toward her breasts, she began to tremble. Sucking air in through her nostrils helped a little. Then he cupped her breasts, holding their weight in his palms, and she didn't care whether she ever breathed again. Didn't care about anything except what his touch did to her.

She felt heavy. Light. Hot and cold, then as if she'd been branded.

Something . . . she should say something. What?

His fingers spread, now pressing her breasts against her, flattening them and drawing them upward, and words were the furthest thing from her mind.

Again she felt as if she'd been weighted with stones. A second later she became weightless—still hot. Becoming hotter.

Cool air laced over her breasts. He'd released her. Maybe he—no. He wasn't done with her. He'd placed his hands on either side of her waist. Slowly, too slowly, he worked his way up her body, bringing her closer to him inch by inch. She answered the call.

With her lips briefly on his, she again found his jeans zipper. This time he didn't try to stop her, and she easily drew it down. The sound of metal against metal momentarily jarred her. Then she again caught the rain's tempo and let that become part of her. Feeling as bold as a storm-driven wind, she drew his jeans down over his hips.

He did nothing to help, leaving her to do the work. She didn't mind. In thoughts, dreams, fantasies, something, she'd done this before. When she'd pushed the jeans down as far as she could without leaning over, she slid out from under his arms, knelt, and finished the task.

Only then did she look at him. All her life she'd known she was any man's equal; she had nothing she needed to prove. This time, this moment, she was willing to put all that behind her and give in to fantasy.

She'd been brought to him. Given to him. He'd bent her before him and now she waited—waited for him to do what he wanted with her.

When he ran his fingers through her hair and pulled her

head back a few inches, she knew he was engaging in the same fantasy. He spread his legs slightly, his swollen sex pressed against his tight, white shorts. Beginning at his calves, hands so hot she thought she might burn him, she inched her way upward, feeling the rough swirls of hair on his thighs, the granite muscles beneath. Because he held her head unmoving, she used her hands to send him wordless messages.

Her fingers were over his hipbones now. Although it had taken a great deal of self-control not to touch him in that most private of ways, she sensed that neither of them was yet ready for that. Still, that didn't mean she couldn't test and tease him as his presence alone did to her.

Sliding her fingers under the tautly stretched elastic band, she began to work his shorts down over his hips. This time he moved in rhythm with her. His grip on her hair became easier. Then, when she'd exposed his manhood, he released her. She could sense him looking down at her, but she kept to her task with suddenly numb fingers. Finally, because he'd kicked off his shoes and socks when they sat down for lunch, he was naked.

Naked.

They were going to make love.

She began to tremble again. Only one thing would put her body at rest. Without meeting his gaze, she raised her hands and he helped her to her feet. It seemed strange to be partially dressed while he was naked, but before she could put her mind to doing anything about it, he freed her of her jeans—once again without touching her flesh. She'd put on a pair of bikini panties this morning—maybe because she had somehow known they were going to wind up like this? Now the few ounces of pale blue lace held his attention.

Standing on legs that trembled almost enough to unbalance her, she waited while he explored her with eyes and hands. Although she desperately wanted to hold him against her, she left her hands resting on his hips, pressing sometimes, while his fingers spread slowly over her belly and hipbones, under the strip of elastic, down, down until she had no choice but to suck in her breath. For a long time she held it, shaking now, body afire.

Still he wasn't done with her. Dropping to his knees, his exploration continued, moving slowly, irrevocably downward. He brought his thumbs together down at the base of her belly and pressed inward. When he did, she clamped her hands over his shoulders, gasped, and arched backward. Because she could hold onto him for support, she managed to stay on her feet. She knew nothing, felt nothing, except his hands.

Lower, drawing inward. Coming closer and closer to what pulsed and ached deep inside her.

When he placed his mouth over her stomach and dampened her flesh with his tongue, the air went out of her lungs as if it had been thrust from her. She fought to stand, but as he rolled her panties down off her legs, she sank beside him on the freshly cleaned throw rug. His body now bracketed her, enveloped her. Surrounded her. She was caught between him and the couch, feeling both trapped and protected. Although she tried to clamp her hands around his neck, he pulled them off him and, holding her wrists prisoner, pushed them behind her and against the couch seat until he'd arched her backward with her breasts thrusting toward him.

She felt his hard knees between hers, felt him pressing closer, forcing her to spread her legs. When she tried to focus on him, she saw nothing except a dark, all-consuming mountain. His swollen sex pressed against her belly, and when he released her wrists, she kept her hands where he'd left them. He moved slightly to one side and caught her right ear between his teeth. She shivered under the teasing assault. Her mouth felt empty; it should be pressed against his.

When she tried to arch forward so she no longer had to support her weight with her arms, he slid away from her. Then he gripped her hips and began to draw her toward him and she understood. While he waited, she straightened her legs so that she was now sitting before him. Gripping her ankles, he pulled her away from the couch. The rug felt cool and silky against her flesh. He wrapped his arms around her, leaned over her, eased her down until she lay looking up at him with her legs on either side of his bent knees.

She saw it in his eyes. The time of waiting, of play, of anticipation, had ended.

Yes, she answered without saying a word.

She couldn't lie still. When he pressed himself between her legs, she lifted her hips to accommodate him. He filled her, slowly, powerfully, and started a rhythm that felt as if it would never end. She didn't want it to end. She began to weep, silent tears coming from so deep within her that she couldn't begin to think how to control them. After that first, frightened second, she no longer tried. Her ignited emotions demanded release and, if this was how, so be it.

Crying, she lost herself in his rhythm. Crying, she let it take control of her.

She stopped trembling, the movement stilled by a new cadence. As she'd done the night they danced, she let the new beat consume her. She felt it in Brand, felt the pulse and drive of his body—joined him.

The room didn't have enough air. Whipping her head away from him, she pulled in enough oxygen that it should have cleared her head. It didn't; she didn't care.

A drum was being beaten, furious tattoos of sound coming from him, from her, from the two of them together.

The sound surrounded her. Consumed her. She joined Brand in his dance and lost herself in the shared tempo.

TEN

"Listen."

Kara rolled her head to one side so her ear was no longer crushed against Brand's arm. After a moment she made sense of what he was calling to her attention. It continued to rain, a gentle but constant rain that danced against the roof and echoed throughout the cabin.

She could put words with the rhythm, maybe create a song for the two of them.

"Isn't that beautiful," she whispered from where she sat nestled beside him on the couch. Songwriting would take too much effort when she simply wanted to exist. He'd slipped back into his jeans, but she couldn't bring herself to getting dressed yet. She gripped the blanket around her instead. "I hope I never tire of hearing that sound."

"A rainy night. Isn't there a song by that name?"

"Maybe you're thinking about Snoopy's dark and stormy night."

Although she was looking out the window at the deep gray, wet world, she could tell he was glaring at her. "I know my rainy nights," he informed her. "And some dog

181

typing on top of his doghouse is not what I had in mind. The truth? Right now, I couldn't care less whether we're able to work tomorrow. Everything's buttoned up; what does one more day matter?''

She knew he wouldn't feel like that much longer, but because she, too, wanted nothing more from life than what she had at this moment, she didn't bother to try to tell either of them differently. They'd had sex—pure and uncomplicated, primitive and unthinking.

They'd also made love. In the midst of that frenzy of need and want, she'd heard *his* heart beating, felt *his* breath against the side of her neck and acknowledged how much she needed those things. She'd cried; no one cried if the emotions weren't involved, did they?

She wished there was someone who could give her the answer.

''Maybe the electricity will go out,'' she said when it occurred to her that he'd been the last to speak.

''The creek might flood. Wash out the bridge.''

''Our trucks won't start. We'll have to stay here as long as there's food in the refrigerator.''

''I've seen your refrigerator. I hate to tell you, but we're going to be in trouble in short order.''

''Okay, so forget the refrigerator. I've got canned goods. How does noodle soup and tuna fish sound?''

He gazed at her for so long that she felt compelled to turn toward him. His features still looked gentled, but his eyes had begun to take on the hue of a stormy afternoon. ''In this world we're painting,'' he whispered, ''there'll never be a phone call.''

She knew he was talking about her father and what lay ahead for all of them. Because she couldn't think of a thing to say, she simply remained beside him. The leg she'd curled under her had gone to sleep, but she couldn't talk herself into moving.

She'd been alone so long, felt alone for her entire life.

Yes, she had a father and brother to love. She'd once received love from her mother. But through all that she'd known she was a separate human being from them.

At this moment she wasn't sure there were any boundaries between her and Brand.

In the distance she heard a hinge squeak and guessed that either Cliff or Ada had stepped out onto their porch. A minute later the hinge protested again.

"They know I'm here," Brand said.

"Does that bother you?"

"Not if it doesn't you."

"It doesn't," she told him. She continued to lean against him for several minutes until she could no longer ignore the pins and needles stabbing at her leg. When she started to shift her weight, his grip on her tightened, until she told him what the problem was. By way of solution, he told her to stretch out on the couch and put her leg on his lap. When she did, barely keeping her blanket around her, he began massaging her calf, her thigh, sometimes pressing against her instep. With her head propped against the couch arm, she rode out the sensations his fingers tapped, once again her world ending with what he was doing to her.

What was taking place inside her.

Because she'd left a window open in the bedroom, the scent of heavy, wet air circled around her. What she pulled into her lungs tasted damp and slightly chilled. Without that for contrast, she would have drowned in Brand's warmth. Maybe she had and simply didn't know when it happened. If so, she didn't mind.

"What are you thiinking?" he asked.

"Nothing."

"Any regrets?"

"Because we made love? No."

She'd only given him a partial answer, but if he wanted more than that, he would have to get it from what he knew about her. When he continued to look at her, she grew uneasy and decided to counter it the only way she knew how. His naked belly was a few inches from her foot. By pointing her toes and scooting closer, she managed to rake her nails lightly against him. He responded as she suspected he would by tightening his muscles there. And by glaring down at her. "Are you asking for trouble?"

"Trouble?" She blinked her lashes at him; at least she gave it her best shot. "I don't know what you're talking about."

"Oh, I think you do." He grabbed her ankle and lifted her foot toward his now open mouth. Although she squirmed, ineffectively gripping the blanket, he clamped his teeth over her big toe. "Stop that, now," he hissed.

"Stop what? I don't know what you're—ow! That hurts."

"It's supposed to hurt. Otherwise, what's the point?"

"You're crazy." Quickly she planted her other foot on his lap and began attacking his stomach with it. His growl of mock rage would have done a grizzly proud, but instead of complimenting him on his acting, she used his momentary distraction to roll off the couch. She landed less than gracefully on the floor, tangled in her covering. Before he could lean over, she scrambled away on hands and knees. She thought she'd gotten away when she felt a tug on her blanket and knew he'd stepped on it.

She kept going. When, with no little effort, she finally managed to get to her feet, she'd surrendered what passed for her clothing. Now she stood naked before him in the cool, damp room with the rain beating out a wordless song against the roof. She needed to put her hands somewhere, anywhere. They wound up planted on her hips and she knew how utterly ridiculous she looked trying to present herself as defiant with her hair hanging down around her and not a stitch of clothing on.

He smiled, a slow, lazy cat, admiring male look. "Come back here," he said.

She should tell him he could take his arrogant order and jump off a tall building with it, but he now held up her underwear for her to see, that self-satisfied cat smile still in place. When she remained firmly planted where her energy had taken her, he dropped the clothes, stood, hooked his thumbs over his waistband, planted his legs far apart, swept his gaze from the top of her head down to her still smarting toe. "Come here, Kara."

No one said a word when she and Brand showed up at work together the next day, but she had no doubt that they were a popular topic of conversation. They shared the same vehicle on Tuesday and Wednesday as well because Brand barely saw the inside of his place during that time. After work on Monday she went with him to the little house he and Chuck rented together. As Brand pulled together a few of his belongings, she made a quick assessment of the place. Obviously it had been built as a rental, and after twenty years of such use, it had seen better days. No wonder he'd rather spend time at her cabin.

Not that insulation, a level floor, and an honest to goodness foundation were the only reasons he'd left Chuck to fend for himself.

During those precious few days when they pretended they were the only two people in the world, she went out of her way not to mention her family. Although she couldn't be sure, she guessed that he, too, worked at avoiding that particular conversation. Instead they jumped into building Cliff and Ada a new porch, cooked together, talked about the day's work, and made love.

When she woke, which she did each night, she pressed herself against Brand's side and refused to ask herself what she was doing with this man. He'd warned her that he occasionally had nightmares, but, next to her, he slept soundly, quietly. She told herself that her presence stood between him and his past.

After work on Thursday, their time away from reality came to an end. Her father had left a message with Cliff and Ada. He and Hank would be flying in tomorrow afternoon.

"Are you sure you know what you're doing?" Ada asked after delivering the message. "What you and Lockwood do is none of my business. Truth is I like seeing you together. Watching you work on the porch was like watching two people with a single mind. But after what you told me, I'd think—well, I don't know what I'd think. I just can't shake the feeling that you're playing with fire."

Kara leaned against the nearest wall and pressed the heel of her hand against her forehead. Because Brand had gone ahead to start a fire in the cabin's wood stove, she felt free to talk. "It shouldn't have happened," she admitted. "I know that. Oh God, do I. But—" She lifted her hands in a helpless gesture. "It's insane. No one has to tell me that. Just because I'm physically attracted to him doesn't—all right, more than just physically attracted."

"More? That isn't enough?"

Knowing Ada was kidding, she went on. "He's intelligent, competent, dedicated—"

"He sounds like the Lone Ranger."

Kara winced at that. "No," she admitted. "Hardly. He's human. He makes mistakes just like the rest of us."

"Like you did getting in over your head with him?"

Ada's question stopped Kara's thoughts. For a moment she simply listened to the words as they vibrated inside her. "I'm in over my head. When I try to explain to myself how this happened, it doesn't make sense. I mean, I believed I would hate him for what he did. I should hate him, shouldn't I? Or at least want nothing to do with him." When Ada didn't answer, she went on. "I tried to tell myself to just walk away from him. To keep distance between us. But I couldn't.''

"Because you fell in love with him.''

Ada had said that before. The first time, Kara had told Ada that she was wrong, told herself she couldn't possibly be doing anything so insane. Now denial wouldn't work. "It shouldn't have happened. I know that; my head does." Again she pressed her hand to her forehead. She kept repeating herself; she had to stop that. "Ada, I always thought I had control over my emotions. I'm not an impulsive person, not . . .''

She stared at the telephone, thinking of her father on the other end of the line and what was going through him at the prospect of seeing Brand Lockwood again. How would he react when he learned that she and Brand had become lovers?

And he would learn because she wasn't going to keep that from him.

"What I feel when I'm around Brand doesn't make sense. All I know is I'm afraid I'll go through life half alive if I'm not with him.''

"Oh honey, you have it bad, don't you?''

Yes, she did, Kara admitted as she stepped into the cabin. Brand closed the stove door and turned toward her. He held out his hands, his eyes steady on her, and she went to him. Without saying a word, she folded herself against him. Whatever *it* was, she had *it* bad.

For a moment she hugged him tightly, feeling his warmth, not what was coming from the stove. *Hold onto me. Don't ever let me go, please.*

"What is it?''

He could tell that much about her? Of course he could. In a voice she wished was stronger, she told him about the message from her father. He nodded and held her gently, firmly. For a long time he said nothing. Then: "How do you feel about it?''

Of all the things he could have said, this had to be the hardest. And the most direct. "Scared. Excited. I want to see my dad. Look at him and see if I can get a reading on how he really feels. And I probably won't believe that Hank is almost recovered until we get into one of our famous wrestling matches. I want to show them some of Skagway. After everything I've told them about it, they'll be expecting it. But, Brand . . ."

"What?" he asked softly.

"You know."

"Yes. I do. But I need to hear it from you."

Suddenly restless, she pulled free and paced over to the bedroom area where she yanked off her boots. Monday after work Brand had picked up a queen-sized mattress from one of the motels and brought it into the cabin. It didn't fit on the old bed frame, but she hadn't minded putting it on the floor. For a few precious days, nothing had mattered except them. And now?

Barely aware of what she was doing, she slipped out of her dirty clothes and put on a robe. She tied the belt tightly around her waist, aware that Brand had been watching the whole time and yet hadn't made a move to touch her.

"I'm going to tell them the truth about us. I owe them that."

"It won't be easy."

"I know." She dropped to her knees and crawled onto the mattress. After a few seconds, she stretched out and spoke to the ceiling. "The first time you and I kissed I knew I couldn't keep it from my family. You'd think knowing what was ahead of me would have been enough to stop me. But . . ." Snatches of the past few weeks slid through her—Brand feeding the wild, cagey dog that hung around the worksite, the care he'd taken to find just the right gift for his mother, his understanding and patience with Cliff and Ada who'd stewed over every aspect of the porch project, the pride he took in his work, concern for the men under him. Most of all she thought about how he hadn't ordered her out of his life and out of a job when she told him who she was.

That was the man she'd fallen in love with. The man she needed her father and brother to get to know.

"I don't want to hurt them," she said to the ceiling. "That's the last thing I'd ever want. But they're going to feel betrayed. I know they will."

"This is going to test your relationship with them in ways it has never been tested before. Ways none of you ever expected."

"Yes." Her voice sounded a little stronger than it had a moment ago. Still, her head pounded so that it hurt to speak. "But there's only one way I can do this—honestly."

"Tell me what to do, Kara. If you want me there, I'll stand beside you. But if you need to be alone with them, I understand."

She rolled onto her side and stared up at him. Despite his serious, wary expression, at that moment she loved him more than she believed possible. And she was terrified that the fragile emotion wouldn't survive the weekend. "They're going to say things—I know they are. I don't want you to have to hear them."

"Will it be any easier facing them on your own?"

"No." The word came out a moan. She tried again. "No. Of course not."

"But it's not something you want to share with me?"

What was he getting at? "You'll know, soon. I'll tell you."

"But we're not enough a part of each other that you're ready to share me with your family."

His words hurt. Still, she knew he'd spoken the truth. "They're a huge chunk of my life, Brand," she told him. "There's never been a moment of my existence that hasn't somehow been tied up with them. You and I—"

"We're new with each other."

New and fragile. "Yes, we are," she admitted.

"We can't change that." He came over and sat beside her on the bed, his weight pulling her toward him. Still, he didn't touch her and she didn't reach out for him. "Things are going to be different for us after this weekend." His voice was soft, low. "What we've had these past few days we'll never have again."

Brand didn't go to the airstrip with Kara when it came time to pick up her relatives. He'd moved his things back to his place, and when Chuck teased him about it, he told his foreman and friend to mind his own damn business. He'd already let Kara know that tonight was for her and her father and brother. He'd see them tomorrow when she brought them up to the worksite.

It came as no surprise when he didn't sleep well and found himself dreading the coming confrontation. Still, because he knew that putting things off would only make it worse, when he saw Art and Hank Crayton get out of the truck with Kara, he walked over to them. Kara's features looked strained, and he wondered how much she'd told them about her personal relationship with him, but he didn't dare focus on her. If he did, his eyes and body language might give away how much she meant to him and how damn scared he was of losing her.

Instead he waited for her to handle the introductions, then held out his hand. For a moment Art simply stared at him, but he finally returned the gesture. Art Crayton's hand had been tempered by a lifetime of physical labor. The flesh felt dry, almost papery, but he hadn't lost any of his strength.

"I thought it would be easier on all of us if we got this over with early," he told Art and Hank. "Right off, I want you to know how much I admire Kara for being honest with me, for insisting I tell her about my role in what's been happening.''

"Yeah." Art glanced over at his daughter. For an instant his features softened, and a work-hardened old man became nothing but a proud and loving father. "I didn't want her to get involved in this mess. I had my reasons. I thought they were powerful reasons. I still do. But Kara's never been one to sit back and let others do the fighting. So, you didn't send her packing. Why not?''

Good question. Brave question. He could tell Art Crayton that his daughter's courage and competence and intelligence and body had turned his life around and made him look at that life in ways he'd never expected, but he didn't. Today wasn't about him. "It isn't my role to judge you, Mr. Crayton. I simply presented my observations and concerns. Why should I deprive your daughter of a job?"

"I'm not sure I believe you play fair. This is a competitive business; we both know that. Put me out of business and that leaves a larger share of the pie for you."

Surely Art didn't believe that. But the man's world had blown up in his face. Maybe even he didn't understand what he was thinking. "I don't operate that way. Never have. Never will. And if you know anything about me, you know that."

Kara hadn't said a word since introducing her father to him. She stood slightly to one side, her body absolutely still. Because Brand had spent nights making love to her and days learning how her mind and heart worked, he believed he understood what was going on inside her.

She was on edge; there was no way she couldn't be. But it hadn't entered her mind to steer the conversation in another, less dangerous, direction. Whatever was said, whatever happened, she would do nothing to alter the course. Another woman might try to defuse the situation by using her femininity, by begging her father to control and contain himself. By sending him silent, warning messages.

But not Kara.

When Art didn't speak, Brand turned toward Kara. She met his gaze, eyes both guarded and accepting. So she took him on his own terms, or at least she did today. How long that would last he couldn't say.

Hank broke the silence. "Tell him, Dad."

"Tell me what?" Brand asked.

Art had been looking at a truck loaded with sheets of styrofoam. Now he squared around toward Brand. "About what just happened. I figure, up here the way you are, you don't knowing what's going on."

"I don't."

"Too bad. The chief investigator, what'd they call him?"

"A diagnostician, Dad."

"Yeah. A diagnostician. He's submitted his report. The results will be made public next week."

Although this was what he'd been waiting for, Brand felt as if he'd been punched. A glance at Kara told him she already knew that. "I see."

"Probably Wednesday," she said. "I'm going to be with Dad when he hears."

Kara hadn't spoken for so long that the sound of her voice caught him off balance. He found himself nodding, even before what she'd said made full sense to him. She wasn't asking for time off work. She was telling him she intended to stand by her family. And she hadn't asked him to be part of that.

He wondered if she was aware of what she'd done.

"Of course," he heard himself say. Then, because they all knew how much rested on what was going to happen on Wednesday and talking wouldn't change anything, he called Art's attention to the styrofoam. He explained that the sheets would be placed over the permafrost so the ice crystals throughout the soil would remain undisturbed. He thought Art might not care, but the older man asked several questions. Hank said nothing. The kid's eyes remained riveted on him.

When Art's questions trailed off, Kara told her father she had to get to work and she'd see him during the lunch break. In the meantime, he and Hank were free to spend as much time looking around as they wanted to. If they ran out of things to do, they could take her truck and come pick her up after work.

She didn't ask Brand if he'd drive her home. He didn't offer.

Kara started for her bulldozer. Art headed toward the styrofoam. Hank, however, didn't move. "You got a minute, Lockwood? This isn't going to take long."

Brand stood his ground, in a way relieved that the time of polite avoidance was over. "I have time," he told the young man, who looked a million times better than the last time he'd seen him. "That's part of why you came up here, isn't it? To talk to me."

"Yeah. It is. First . . ." Hank folded his arms. At least he tried to. His forearms were so muscular that they got in the way of the gesture. That's why he'd healed as fast as he had. Because he was young and healthy and strong— like his sister. "First, I want to thank you for saving my life. I'm not sure you would have done it if you'd known who I was."

"I knew. You told me your name."

"I did?" Hank looked puzzled. "And you didn't leave me where I was?"

"I'd never be able to face myself if I did that." Kara had returned. Now she stood near her brother, once again not moving, not trying to interfere. Art was still close enough that he, too, could hear.

"Maybe." Hank spat out the word. "I don't know

what's going on inside you, Lockwood. How you can save my life one minute and try to ruin my dad's the next?''

"It isn't like that. Don't you understand, none of this is as simple as any of us wants it.''

"It's pretty cut and dried to me. You've put my father out of business. Maybe destroyed him. That's something I'll never forget.''

Brand hoped to God the kid never did. Someday Hank might have his own business and the kind of responsibilities Brand—and Art—had learned to shoulder. At the core of those responsibilities had to be concern for the human beings dependent on him for their livelihoods and safety. "I made a judgment call by presenting what I did. Even—'' He glanced at Kara; he couldn't help himself. "No matter what happens on Wednesday, I'll never regret what I did.''

Hank's eyes flickered from Brand to Kara, then back to Brand again. "Never regret? Even if they say my dad's guilty?''

"Would you rather I kept my mouth shut? What if the accident was glossed over and it happened again? Could any of us live with that?'' He wasn't going to touch Kara. He didn't dare and, even if he did, she wouldn't want it. But he felt himself sliding a few inches closer to her, looking at her again; he couldn't stop himself. "This isn't a matter of taking sides, Hank. It—''

"No. It sure as hell isn't.''

Kara sucked in her breath but didn't say anything. Brand forced himself to concentrate on Hank. "Kara knows what my concerns were, what I said to the investigators. I assumed she relayed that to you.''

"She did. Only, it looks like that's all she told us. Look, Lockwood, this is awkward as hell for me. I just want you to know that. You save my life, then turn around and maybe destroy my father's. I don't know how I'm supposed to feel.''

You aren't the only one. "I understand." Someone was starting up a cement truck. The sound of concrete being turned inside the massive drum made conversation all but impossible. "Believe me, I understand."

"You're sleeping with him, aren't you?"

The accusation hit Kara with the force of a blow to her heart. Still, when she faced her brother who'd been staring at the queen-sized mattress on the floor, she managed to keep her emotions under control. "Yes. I am."

Hank hadn't expected her to say that. Confusion beat out the look of pain in his eyes. "Why? Damn it, sis. Why?"

Because I can't have it any other way. "That's my business, Hank."

"I don't think so." Hank had plopped his muscular body onto the couch in her cabin, the one she'd shared with Brand a few short nights ago. "Look, sis, I never thought I'd have to say this, but it smells to me as if you sold Dad out."

Was he trying to hurt her as retaliation for what he believed she'd done to their father? If so, he'd succeeded. "It's not as simple as that." Why was this so hard? She'd known she'd have to explain. "Nothing about this is simple."

"Tell me about it!" Hank leaned toward their father. "Didn't you catch the vibes, Dad? Those two have the hots for each other."

"Hank!" No. She wasn't going to lose her temper. Only, he had no call making what she and Brand had sound dirty. *Had? Maybe.* "Look—" She walked over to where her father was sitting silently in an ancient rocking chair and knelt beside him. She took his hands in hers, feeling his strength and age. "Dad, I came here believing I'd hate Brand. No. Not hate." How was she going to make her family understand if she didn't herself? "After what he did for Hank, I can't hate him. But I never thought I'd respect him, or—"

"Or fall into bed with him," Hank interjected.

If she didn't love her brother so much, she would have slapped him. "It's all so simple for you, isn't it?" she challenged. "For you, everything's black or white."

"I've been with Dad every day of this hell. You haven't."

Hank was right about that. "I know," she acknowledged. "Do you think my not being there was easy? But there were certain things I believed I had to do." She squeezed her father's hand. "Because this proud, stubborn man was trying to bottle everything up inside him."

When Hank didn't immediately lash back at her, she guessed that he'd spent some of his initial anger. Still, he was a long way from understanding. Only, because she barely understood her emotions when it came to Brand, she didn't know what to say.

After a minute, she rocked to her feet and walked over to the sink for a glass of water. Returning, she leaned against a wall. "Life's so complicated. The older I get, the more I believe that. What happened? That's what you want to know, isn't it?" When Hank nodded, she went on. "I've been watching Brand. I've seen the way he conducts himself. I admire his code of ethics."

"Admire? What about your ethics, sis?"

She loved her brother; she would always love him. That didn't mean there weren't times—like now—when she could barely stand to stay in the same room with him. "If you don't know the answer to that, then you don't know me."

When Hank pressed the heel of his hand hard against his thigh, she knew she'd gotten through to him.

"I don't want to fight with you," she said. "And Dad, I don't want to hurt you." She pushed away from the wall and paced, feeling heavy, toward the window. With her back to her brother and still silent father, she stared out at the wilderness. A few days ago she'd looked out this same window and watched it rain. Then she'd turned back to the man she'd just made love to and asked him to take over her world again.

It had been so simple back then.

Still facing the window, she went on. "I didn't want to care for him. Right after I told him who I was, he became so angry that the last thing I wanted was to have to be in the same state with him. But . . ." Why was she doing this? Love wasn't something that could easily be turned into words. Love wasn't practical, rational. Most of all it wasn't wise.

"Dad? Please. Tell me what you're thinking."

When he remained silent, she faced him. He seemed to have shrunken, a suddenly old man sitting in a rocking chair. Frightened by the thought, she hurried across the room, this time to stand behind him so she could wrap her arms around him and press her cheek against the back of his head. This man had molded and shaped her life.

What she felt for Brand Lockwood was new, untested.

"I can't dictate what you feel, honey," her father said at last. "I've only really been in love once and it was a long time ago. What I had with your mother was good, so good that I guess it lasted me for my whole life. But when we got married, it was with everyone's blessing."

She almost told him that marriage had never come up between her and Brand, but that wasn't what this was about. Hank continued to watch her; for one of the few times in her life, she didn't know what her brother was thinking. "I wish Mom was here," she whispered. "I need to talk to her."

"I wish she was, too, honey. All I know is—" her father wrapped his hand over hers, "the way things are now, what you just told me, I don't want to have to talk to Lockwood. I need my daughter to understand that."

ELEVEN

Because is was Sunday, Kara was able to spend the entire day with her brother and father. Still, when she took them back to the airstrip late that evening and waved them off, it was with a sense of relief. She wouldn't be surrounded by her father's tension and her brother's still simmering anger, until she flew down to be with them after work on Tuesday.

All Sunday, at least, they'd put the topic of Brand Lockwood behind them, and she introduced them to some of what she'd discovered about Skagway. Maybe they understood that she'd told them all she could about what she felt for Brand. And maybe neither of them cared to try to bridge the undeniable gap that now existed between the three of them.

I'm sorry, Dad, she thought as the little plane banked and headed south. *I didn't want this to happen. I never planned it. Never.*

Brand was waiting for her when she returned home. When she first saw him, she simply sat in her truck and let the steering wheel support her forearms. The world had ceased to exist when they were together. For a few precious days and nights she'd—they'd—pretended that they were like any other couple caught up in the simple magic of being with each other.

Only, they weren't any other couple. It was time to face that.

"I don't know if you want company or not," he said as he helped her from her truck. He slid his hands along her waist, hugged her briefly, then let her go. His eyes locked with hers. "If not, just say the word and I'll leave."

She needed to be alone. And yet she needed him even more. Without answering him, she walked away from him and stepped inside the cabin, leaving the door open so he could follow her. Feeling drained, she turned on her stereo and selected a country and western tape. The singer was a woman; in a soft, lilting voice she sang of a love that survived the years. Still not speaking, Kara collapsed on the couch. Brand joined her. Their bodies didn't touch.

"Do you want to talk?"

"No." She should have taken an aspirin first. "Not about that."

For too long he simply regarded her. Then, without asking permission, he pulled her around so that she was facing him. Before she could think to ask what he was doing, he removed her shoes and then drew off her socks. He pressed his thumbs against the ball of her right foot, the massage instantly, miraculously wiping tension from her body. After a few seconds, she rested her head against the back of the couch. What did it matter? They'd gone too far to pretend nothing had happened between them, even if she wanted to. "I don't know why I'm so tired." She little more than mouthed the words. "We didn't do that much walking. Wandering, ambling, riding the buckboard twice."

"Kara. Being tired physically has nothing to do with

how you feel. The past few days haven't been easy. The strain's bound to tell.''

''I don't want to talk about them.''

''So you said. I'll respect that, for now. But we're going to have to, soon.''

Not her but *we*. The simple word clogged her throat. ''I know. Only—I don't think Dad likes flying. He's never said, but he always gets quiet and short tempered just before he boards a plane. Hank loves it. When he was a boy, he had pictures of jets and fighter planes and helicopters all over his walls. Maybe someday he'll be able to get a pilot's license.''

When he asked if she knew where Hank's love of aircraft had come from, she told him about her brother flying to a work site with their father when he was no more than five or six years old. Although she spun out the story in slow, exacting detail, he barely listened to the words.

The past two days were at the top of the list as the hardest in his life. Although he'd kept his vow to distance himself from Kara while her family was here, his thoughts and heart had been with her the entire time. He'd been aware of Hank watching him and Kara that morning on the mountain and guessed Hank had sensed something— some energy, vibes, something—between them.

Had her brother called her on that, not given her the opportunity to tell them the way she wanted to? If so, Kara had had to weather her brother's accusations alone. He wanted to ask her about that and encourage her to share her reaction with him. But she'd told him she didn't want to talk about the ways his life had become woven in with her family's, and he had no choice but to respect that.

She'd closed him out.

Again.

''We should have taken pictures,'' she finally said.

''What?'' Had he missed something?

"When you and I were on the narrow-gauge. Why didn't we think to take along a camera?"

Because you were all I could concentrate on. "Maybe next time."

"Maybe."

She sounded wistful. Concern for her carved its way between him and his unanswerable question of what Wednesday would bring. Would do to them. "Maybe you'd rather charter a plane and explore some of the glaciers. If you want, I'll see if we can reserve one for next Sunday."

"I might not be back."

Her words pounded at him; insanely, he wanted to pound back. "I need you here, Kara. We've got a job to do."

Her mouth thinned, became firmer than he'd ever seen it. "I know; you don't have to tell me that. Divided loyalties, they've been tearing me apart."

"It sounds as if you've made your decision."

"Decision? I wish it was as simple as that. Brand, I have to know what shape my father's in, whether he's going to be indicted. That comes first. It has to."

He stopped massaging her foot. Suddenly he wanted to get up and walk out of the cabin. If he'd been Hank's age, he probably would have. But her words had made their impact; damn it, he understood her struggle. Hurt for her. "They're always going to come first, aren't they?" he made himself ask.

"Maybe." She sounded exhausted. "I don't know." Before he could think what, if anything, he wanted to say, she stood and padded barefoot over to the living room window. With her back to him, he couldn't tell enough of what was going on inside her.

He wasn't sure he wanted to know, or if he could handle feeling anything more than he already did.

"I wish I'd never come to Skagway."

"Do you?" He felt a sharp pain in his knee and looked down. If he hadn't been wearing jeans, his short, strong nails would have torn flesh. As it was, he knew he'd inflicted a bruise on himself.

"No." She spun around but with the light behind her, he couldn't see enough of the message in her eyes. "I didn't mean that."

He didn't want to get any closer to her than he was. When he got to his feet it was, he thought, with the intention of leaving. Instead he wound up standing in front of her, his hands reaching for her. She backed away, and then he did the same.

"I don't want to make love with you." She whispered the words.

"Did I ask?"

Her mouth sagged, and he knew he'd wounded her. "I'm sorry," he apologized. "I didn't mean for it to come out like that."

"Didn't you? Oh, Brand, I don't know what I'm thinking half the time. Sometimes I just want to go someplace where I can scream until I'm hoarse. Then—" The faintest of wistful smiles touched her mouth. "Then I want to curl up on the couch and have you massage my feet and tell me . . . Most of all I don't want any of this to be happening."

"Neither do I."

When she shifted her weight, the gesture bringing her a few inches closer to him, he again extended his hands, even though he knew how unwise the gesture was. But she placed hers in his. They stood there, hands laced together, arms swinging slightly, breathing. Simply breathing.

"I was wrong," she whispered.

"About what?"

"What I said a minute ago. I want to make love." Her eyes remained locked with his. "I need to. If you—"

"Don't say a word." Stepping still closer, he ran his

hands up her arms and felt her shiver. "It's better if we don't."

Had that been her? Kara asked as she listened to the hum of an airplane engine. She'd always believed herself brave, taken great pride in that. But last night she'd sounded wounded and scared. And needful.

Below her, the little town of Skagway became less distinct and then faded off into nothing. The mountains, heavy and white-capped, seemed to surround her despite the plane's altitude. It had been night when she first flew into Skagway, and she hadn't been hit with the full impact of how totally the mountains dominated the landscape. Now she could put her mind to their majesty.

She'd gotten the call this morning. The hearing was tomorrow—Tuesday. *I might not come back.* She'd told Brand that, but now, feeling the mountains reach out to claim her, the wrench of leaving nearly tore her in two.

He hadn't seen her off. He couldn't; a problem at work had held him there.

Blinking back tears, she told herself it was better that way. With her emotions tangled around her, she wouldn't have been able to say a word to him.

Maybe three words. *I love you.*

There were four other passengers in the plane, local residents on their way to Anchorage for business or pleasure. The pilot had just told them that this was his third flight of the day, and he was glad he didn't have any tourists on board this time. How anyone worked full time as a tour guide he didn't know. Too many questions.

As one of the men started a story about having to help repair a broken-down tour bus, Kara concentrated on the world outside the plane. She could make out the dark ribbon of water known as the Lynn Canal. What was it she'd said to Brand? That she couldn't imagine sailing on it without being acutely aware of how isolated this part of the world was.

But when, or if, she returned, it wouldn't matter to her that Skagway existed apart from much of the world—because Brand would be there.

She was getting melancholy. That's all it was, depression brought on by too many nights without enough sleep.

And what might happen tomorrow.

And what that would do to what she and Brand had begun.

Why hadn't he known?

Even as she searched for her father and brother in the Anchorage airport, the question echoed in her mind. There were two answers, one simple, one the most complex of her life.

He had a job to do and wasn't free to leave.

What she was going through didn't concern him enough.

She tried to tell herself that wasn't it, that their silent, wonderful lovemaking should be all the proof she needed to believe that he'd seen inside her heart—that he understood.

But if he did, he would be here now. Wouldn't he?

Hank's welcoming shout took her from her thoughts. She hurried over to her family, threw her duffle bag at her brother, and engulfed her father.

"What am I? Some kind of pack animal?" Glowering, Hank hoisted his burden over his shoulder.

"That's about it. Be glad you're good for that." With her arm around her father's solid waist, she tried a smile on her brother. The duffle bag was all she'd brought. Even if she decided to stay here with her family, she'd have to go back for the rest of her belongings, dispose of her truck, and say good-bye to Cliff and Ada.

See Brand.

"So—" She turned her attention to her father. "Did you take my advice and get yourself a new pair of shoes?"

Art stuck out his foot so she could see the clean white tennis shoes. "What advice? That was as close to an order as I've ever heard."

"So?" She shrugged. "Any man who runs around with his toes hanging out needs someone to get him back on track." As they headed toward her father's truck, still arguing about shoes, the reality of what he'd chosen struck her. Her father had always worn boots; she'd almost never seen him in anything else.

Not any more.

The house needed a little TLC in the way of cleaning, but considering everything that had been going on, the two bachelors hadn't done a half bad job of keeping things up. That had always been an unspoken family rule. Just because she was the woman didn't mean that all the house-work fell on her shoulders.

"You haven't forgotten what it's like to have an honest to goodness kitchen, have you?" Hank teased as he handed her a glass of iced tea. "I'm not sure what you call yours."

"Kitchen area," she emphasized. "It's the latest thing. Total efficiency."

"Totally useless, you mean. You haven't said. How long are you going to be here?"

Kara told her brother she didn't know. It depended, she said, on what happened tomorrow.

"What does your boss say?"

"My boss—" Although she hadn't intended to, she wound up drawing out the word. "Didn't say much. I told him I was going to do what I had to."

Her father nodded but didn't say anything. Instead, he gave his full attention to his drink. After a minute he walked over to the answering machine and punched a button. There were two messages, one from the consulting firm he'd been working for. They thanked him and called his report complete, then said they didn't think they'd need him for at least a month. The other message was from the attorney he'd hired. The lawyer would meet them just inside the courthouse a little before the scheduled meeting.

Her father sank into his chair, glanced at his spotless shoes, met her eyes. "Well, I guess that's that."

Although she wanted to beg him not to sound so depressed, a different tone of voice wouldn't erase what he felt inside. She hurried over to him and knelt before him. Placing her hands on his knees, she met his eyes. "We'll get through it. I promise you."

By 9:30 the next morning, Kara had resigned herself to whatever the outcome might be. Her almost unthinking calm surprised her, but maybe, after the weeks of uncertainty, she was simply relieved to know it would soon all be over.

Her father and brother seemed to feel the same way. Although they'd said little as they got ready for the hearing, she sensed only a minimum of tension in the air.

The phone didn't ring. Although she told herself Brand wouldn't have had time to call her before leaving for work, she didn't really believe it. She kept asking herself what she'd say to him if she heard his voice on the line.

In the end she was left not knowing.

"I thought *he* might get in touch with you," Hank said as they drove over to the county courthouse where the meeting, hearing, whatever the officials called it, would be held. "But maybe the two of you got it all said beforehand."

We didn't get anything said. Not bothering to answer her brother, Kara gave her father's shoulder a squeeze. "You're looking pretty handsome this morning. All dressed up—we might have to chase the ladies away."

Art fingered his new shirt collar, then squeezed closer to the truck door so she'd have a little more room inside the cab. "They're all going to be wearing suits," he grumbled. "I thought about buying one, but how I'm dressed isn't going to change anything."

No, it isn't, Kara thought. Although she wanted to go on touching her father, she sensed that he needed to be alone with whatever was going through him.

It was the same for her. Only, her mind refused to settle on what would happen this morning. No matter how many times she tried to keep thoughts of Brand from taking over, he refused to leave her alone.

He should have called; he owed her that much.

After parking, Kara, her father, and brother started walking toward the multistory building. Even though she didn't look back at the truck, the red and white lettering on both doors was embedded in her mind. *Crayton Construction.* After today, would the words be a lie?

Just before they reached the door, Art grabbed Hank's arm. Kara stopped, alarmed by the look on her father's face.

"Dad? What is it? Don't you feel well?"

"Forget how I feel. There's something I have to say to both of you before we go in there."

Although she and Hank exchanged glances, neither of them spoke. Still holding onto his son, Art began. "I've gone over it in my mind a thousand times, looking at things from every angle I can think of. It hasn't been easy admitting Lockwood might have been right, that my not being on top of technology was responsible for the collapse."

Kara wanted to tell her father that Brand didn't know. He had simply suggested that as a possible cause. Instead, she remained silent.

"I don't see it. That's what's been keeping me awake nights. I honestly can't think of a thing I should have done differently. Damn it, I've done this kind of work all my life. I didn't do anything different this time. I didn't."

"I know that, Dad."

Art gave his son a sideways glance and an appreciative smile. "That's not what I want to talk about." For a moment he stared down at the only pair of dress shoes he owned, then focused on Kara. "You look so pretty today. Sometimes when I see you, I think your mama's still alive."

With an effort, Kara kept her hands out of the pockets of her white slacks and away from the pale yellow rayon blouse she'd worn only once before. If her father continued to talk like that, she didn't know how she could keep from crying.

"You should have dresses, dress pretty, have your hair done."

"Dad, I don't want those things."

"I know you don't," he said softly. "Still—I am so proud of you two. I just want you to know that. I don't deserve you."

"The hell you don't, Dad," Hank said, his tone rough. "Don't ever start thinking that."

"I can't help it. What I put you two through, thinking I had to handle this on my own, I wouldn't blame you if you both told me to go hang myself."

"We'd never do that. You know that." Kara made fists of her hands.

"I do know that. Now." A trio of men in business suits stepped outside. For a moment their voices filled the air, and then they were gone.

"I let my pride get in the way, couldn't admit to my own kids that I couldn't handle this by myself. Kara, you had to go to Lockwood for answers that should have come from me. Honey, Hank, I'm sorry."

Mindless of anyone who might see, Kara hugged her father. A thousand words and emotions filled her, but if a heartfelt embrace didn't say everything, then nothing else would. When she finally forced herself to release her father, her brother first clasped Art's hand, then pulled him roughly against him.

A full minute later, Hank opened the heavy glass door and the three of them stepped inside. The lawyer Art had retained was waiting for them. After shaking hands with Kara, he explained that the hearing would be held in a meeting room in the city planning department. The time for the hearing, unfortunately, had been made public which meant the press would be there.

Although the only thing she wanted to do was grab her father and brother and run, Kara led the way into the dark, crowded room. Space had been left for them at one end of the rectangular table. She sat down on the opposite side of the lawyer from her father and forced herself not to give her father an encouraging smile. A TV camera crew had set up their lights and camera. If they were already filming, she wanted to present a picture of confidence, not fear.

Brand! I need you.

Not knowing what to expect, she could only wait for someone to begin. Once everyone was seated, the middle-aged man at the head of the table stood and introduced himself as Sidney Rembert, senior city engineer. Although she needed to concentrate on his every word, she couldn't keep her eyes off the piles of material in front of him. So that's what the past few weeks had been about—filling out these reports and studies.

"As way of introduction," Mr. Rembert began, "I want to say that I'd hoped the probe could have been completed before this. Granted, there were a great many aspects to cover. Still, now that we have our results, I'm sorry we were unable to focus on that particular issue from the beginning."

Kara wanted to scream at the engineer to get on with

it. At the same time, she would have given a great deal to be able to get up and walk out of the room—taking her father and brother with her.

Brand?

Mr. Rembert braced himself against the table. "I'm willing to wager that it simply isn't possible to conduct a more thorough investigation than what's been accomplished here. Let me assure you—" He nodded at Art and his attorney, "that everything has been gone over with a fine-toothed comb. I'm certain everyone in this room will agree that none of us ever wants anything like this to happen again. That's why we were determined to examine all aspects."

He went on, his words both clipped and droning. Although she struggled to concentrate, so far Mr. Rembert really hadn't said anything. Next to her, she sensed Hank moving restlessly. Keeping her hand under the table where no one could see, she clamped her fingers over his knee. She felt his muscles tense, but after a few seconds his breathing slowed.

"What is this?" he whispered. "A political speech?"

If so much didn't ride on Mr. Rembert's words, she might have laughed.

"The total cost of this process has exceeded $100,000. Believe me, the advice of experts does not come cheap. Fortunately, Mr. Crayton had adequately insured his project and the expenses we've incurred were picked up by the insurer." Mr. Rembert held aloft a thick folder. "This contains an item-by-item documentation of every expenditure and will be made available to the press. In addition, it will remain part of the city's permanent record. I anticipate requests for it from other entities conducting their own investigations."

"I don't care."

Although she couldn't agree more, Kara didn't acknowledge her brother's hissed comment. The TV newsman, young and handsome, every hair in place, glanced at his watch and then whispered something to the man handling the camera. The cameraman grinned. Kara wanted to yell at the two that there was nothing funny about this.

She wanted Brand here.

Shaking off thoughts, memories, images, she leaned forward. Mr. Rembert wore a gray-blue dress shirt and dark blue tie. Although the knot at his throat had been expertly tied, the tie had somehow caught on a shirt button. Why, she wondered, did she find that so interesting?

"The preliminaries dispensed with," he continued. "it's time to get on to the meat of why we're here."

She heard Hank draw in his breath. Or maybe it was herself she heard.

"There is a cause, a single, indisputable one. For a long time we thought this might simply be a contributing factor, that there might be other elements involved, but after thorough investigation—"

You already said that.

"We have concluded that the steel girders used were improperly manufactured."

Mr. Rembert's mouth continued to open and close. The handsome TV man was writing furiously and the camera swung from the engineer to her father, then back to the engineer again. She felt Hank's muscles contort and stay hard.

Improperly manufactured steel girders.
Nothing Dad had any control over.
Nothing he could have foreseen.

"All right!" Hank cheered, and then hissed into Kara's ear, "Damn him. All this hell for nothing."

_____ TWELVE _____

Hank gripped her arm and yanked. His effort nearly made her lose her balance.

"Damn it, sis, you know why the stupid investigation took so long."

Kara glared at her brother. Because her father and his lawyer were tied up talking to the press, she and Hank had managed to break free and find an unused room for their confrontation. "Go on," she challenged. "Tell me."

"Because of Lockwood. He pointed the finger at Dad. For too damn long, they focused on areas Dad had control over. If they'd started looking where they should have . . ." Although he continued to hold onto her, his grip slackened until it no longer hurt. "Tell him that. When you go back to _him,_ tell him Dad didn't have to go through hell."

Hank was speaking out of emotion. After he'd had time to calm down, he'd understand that every aspect of the project had to be examined. That even if the substandard girders had been discovered at the beginning, the search for contributing causes would have continued. She tried to tell him that. Before she half had the words out, he shook his head.

"I don't buy it, sis. Okay, granted, they had to go through the motions. But damn it, they didn't have to treat our father as if he was a criminal. They wouldn't have if Lockwood hadn't said what he did."

"We don't know that." Hank had released her. Not caring what he might think, she massaged her forearm. "Hank, please, we shouldn't be fighting. Not now."

When he blinked and rocked backward a few inches, she knew she'd gotten through to him. She could also remind him that he might be dead if it hadn't been for Brand, but he knew that.

Still, she understood his anger. Brand's role in all this, his suspicions, the way those suspicions colored his words, had to have an impact on the investigators.

He should be here.

She didn't know when she'd go back to Skagway, what she'd do and say once she got there.

She told Hank they had to get back to their father or he would start wondering where they'd gone. Her brother opened the door he'd slammed shut a few minutes ago and stood back to let her go out first. As she started down the hall, he touched her back. Without looking at him, she stopped and waited. "What are you going to say to him?" he asked.

"Dad?"

"No. Brand."

Brand. Her brother hadn't called him that before. "I don't know." She turned. "We left everything—so unsettled."

Hank nodded, his eyes now calm, sad even. "This is harder on you than anyone else, isn't it? Caught in the middle the way you are."

She blinked back sudden tears. Could Hank guess how much she needed someone to talk to, to help her sort out her emotions?

Only this wasn't the time for that. When they reentered the meeting room, the TV crew was putting away its equipment and most of the members of the investigative committee had already left. When her father glanced at her, she could tell he knew what she and Hank had talked about. She thought he might say something about it. Instead, with the lawyer standing beside him, her father explained that he'd just learned that his contractor's license would be released to him, the day after tomorrow at the latest.

"Dad, that's wonderful!" Suddenly she sobered. "What are you going to do with it?"

"Bid on a couple of jobs. Small ones. Middle of the season like this, I wouldn't be able to get my full crew back."

Kara nodded, heartened by the enthusiasm in his voice. Already he looked less tired, younger than he had lately. It wouldn't take long before news of his acquittal, if that's what it was called, spread throughout the contracting community. As soon as his crew had finished the jobs they'd gone to, they'd return to him.

How long would it be before Brand knew?

Did he care enough to call Anchorage, or would he wait until she told him?

Of course he cared. Hadn't his lovemaking taught her what she needed to know about his compassion?

Compassion? If he understood her need, he would be here. Or if he couldn't, he would have phoned, sent flowers, something. Flowers? Did she want that from him?

Hank was saying something about how Art had kept abreast of the two projects he was interested in as they went through the planning stages and shouldn't have much trouble working up accurate bids. She tried to match their enthusiasm, even smiled in the appropriate places.

Inside she felt dead.

"This calls for a celebration," Hank announced. "Since none of us was in the mood for breakfast, I suggest we go somewhere where we can put on the feed buckets. Of course—" he gave her a half teasing, half serious look, "since at the moment my sister is the one with the big money around here, it's only right that she have to foot the bill."

Kara assured him she'd be happy to do that. However, she expected to be paid back, with double-digit interest. As she spoke, she fought to keep from thinking. That might be the only way she'd get through the day.

Silence was the worst thing Brand could have given her.

When they stepped outside, she had to squint against the sunlight glinting off a car top. She fought a memory, denied it. Still it returned.

The sun had shown rich and full the day Brand and his crew worked on Cliff and Ada's bridge. She remembered the simple pleasure of studying the few harmless clouds.

She remembered going into her cabin with Brand later and closing the door between them and the world. They hadn't made love then; they hadn't been ready for that.

But the promise had been there.

Promise?

The word was a lie.

Squinting, she was able to make out her father's truck with *Crayton Construction* painted on the side. The lettering wouldn't have to come off after all.

"You all right?" her father asked. He slipped his arm around her shoulder, reminding her of how many times he'd done that through the years when she needed a comforting presence.

"I'll survive" was the best she could come up with. She gave herself a shake. No matter what wasn't right between her and Brand, she wouldn't ruin today for her father.

She started to tell him that she'd been thinking about the company logo when Hank, who was on her other side, touched her shoulder. He pointed. She followed the line of his finger.

Brand. Standing on a grassy strip between two parking areas.

Keep walking, a voice deep inside warned. *Let him think you got through this without him.*

She couldn't make her legs work.

. "Honey?" It was her father. "Go talk to him. We'll be in the truck."

No! I don't want to be with him. You—this is family time. Still, a strength she didn't understand propelled her toward Brand. A moment later, she heard the truck door slam.

"What are you doing here?"

"I had to be here for you." He wore flannel and denim, worn work boots.

She didn't know who this uncertain woman in white slacks and a silky-feeling blouse was. If she continued to stand on pavement, he would go on towering over her. She stepped up on the grass, careful to keep her distance from her boss. The lawn had been mown recently, maybe this morning. The clean, rich scent mingled with that of Brand's aftershave. He had come to her.

She wanted him.

"He was acquitted. Exonerated," she said. "Whatever. It wasn't his fault."

"I know."

He knew? And yet he was still here, waiting for her. "How?"

"I called the chief engineer right after I landed this morning. He was still at home. He said, well, you know what he said."

Brand had flown in earlier today? That's why he hadn't called.

"Did it surprise you?" She hated the sharp tone in her voice, but she still carried Hank's words inside her.

Her words as well.

"I told you. It wasn't my place to make judgments."

"Right." She spat out the word. "You simply pointed the finger. It nearly cost my father his career, his health, his self-esteem, but . . ." *Stop*. Still, she opened her mouth, thinking she needed to get the rest of the words out.

Stop.

He was too big. She needed him to be less—less everything. When he went on looking at her, eyes dark and deep, she realized he was waiting for her to say everything she'd been holding inside.

But there wasn't anything.

Nothing except the humming of her body. The heat of her.

"How is he?"

She tried to guess how long they'd been staring at each other, but time had looped back upon itself and she was caught in the knot.

"Relieved. It hasn't all sunk in yet I'm sure. Hungry. He's hungry."

"I want to talk to him, soon. And your brother. There're things all of us need to say."

"Yes. There are. But—"

"But what? Kara, maybe once we've said what we need to, we can all start over. I'd like to try." He glanced at the truck. "Tell them to go get something to eat."

"I said I'd go with them."

"Later. They had you this morning. Now it's my turn."

My turn. The words made her weak; she marshalled her forces against that. "You knew before we did. Do you have any idea what the waiting was like for us?"

"Yeah. I think I do."

Where was her anger? She needed the emotion; it would give her something to feel. Or maybe the truth was, anger was far safer than what she was experiencing. She searched through her mind for snatches of what Hank had thrown at her when they were alone, but she'd lost the words.

She'd never have them back again.

"Why didn't you call after you found out?" She sounded as if she was inquiring about the weather.

He didn't answer. At least not right away. Instead, he waved at her family, indicating they could leave. She thought Hank might ask if that was what she wanted. Instead, she heard the truck start up and then drive away.

"I wanted to," Brand said. "You must know that. But Rembert wouldn't let me; he said that was his role."

"He did?"

Brand nodded, his eyes telling her how much his silence had cost him. "You look beautiful this morning."

"What?"

"Yellow is a good color for you. And your hair down like that—you're beautiful."

She fingered the blouse, touched her hair. "I am?"

By way of answer, he slid his hands into his back pockets. Strangely, she felt like laughing. *You do that whenever you're working things out in your mind,* she almost told him.

"Kara? I want you to know something. Not coming down with you yesterday was the hardest thing I've ever done."

With his words, the strength went out of her legs. Unmindful of her white slacks, she lowered herself to her knees and then scooted around until she was sitting with her legs folded in front of her. Before she had to stare up at him, Brand joined her. Now his hands rested on his thighs, a hard-working man's hands stretched over denim.

"Why didn't you?" she asked.

"Because that time was for you and your family. And because I told myself you needed to be away from me."

Her stomach knotted. "You did?"

"To decide how you feel about me."

Didn't he know? But how could he when what she felt was tangled deep inside her? She leaned forward, thinking to rest her elbows on her legs. The thick carpet of grass caught her attention. She ran her hand over it, feeling its lush dampness. "Why didn't you tell me that?"

"Why?" He laughed the word, then sobered. "Kara, don't you understand, I needed time, too."

He did? The thought of the conclusions he might have come to scared her. "I wanted you there today. I kept thinking . . ." When he started to speak, she held up her hand, stopping him. "But that time was for my family. Having you there would have only distracted them . . . us . . . me . . . from what we needed to concentrate on. You understand, don't you?"

He nodded.

"But I felt lost without you. I tried to tell myself I didn't. It was a lie."

"Why?"

"Why did I lie to myself?" She felt dampness under her and wondered if the grass had strained her slacks. If she'd been wearing jeans it wouldn't matter. "I don't know." No. That wasn't the truth. "Self-preservation."

She thought he might recoil from the words. Instead he nodded. "That's a large part of why I didn't come with you," he told her. "Self-preservation."

What was he saying? She tried to hold onto the question and give it definition, but he'd stood up and was extending his hand to her. She felt his fingers close down around hers and then, without being aware of how it had been accomplished, she was standing beside him.

"I have to go back tonight," he said.

"Do you?" Of course he did. His job demanded that. Without her? How would she survive hearing that?

"Come with me. Please."

Please. The word had been spoken so softly that the

gentle breeze nearly bore it away. She caught it and held it against her. "You want—"

"Not want, Kara. I need you. That's what I learned last night—during my time alone."

Before he'd finished speaking, he slid his arm around her. Holding her in front of him, he did nothing more than look down at her. She felt his warm breath as he exhaled.

He hadn't said anything about not being able to get the job done if he was short a heavy equipment operator. If he had, she could have kept her equilibrium. But he'd said he needed *her* and something in her chest began to swell.

"Tonight?" she whispered. "With you?"

"If that's what you want."

What was it he'd told her a moment ago, that he'd remained in Skagway last night because self-preservation was important to him. Only, he'd just said he *needed* her.

"I don't know what to say," she whispered.

"Neither do I. But I'm going to try. I have to. The things I thought about when I was alone . . ."

"What things?" she prompted.

"You're ready for this? You might not want to hear it." When she said nothing, he went on. "I want you to think back a few days. When you learned that the results would be made public today, you *told* me you were going to be with your family. You didn't ask for time off work; you didn't ask me to come with you. I tried to convince myself—" With his free hand, he pushed a strand of hair off her forehead. "I told myself you didn't need me. That we hadn't become that important to each other. I was wrong."

"Wrong?" Why was she doing this, hiding behind questions when he deserved to know everything about her—everything that mattered. "I'm sorry," she whispered. "So sorry. I should—I thought—when I knew what was going to happen today, I was afraid to let you know how much I wanted you with me."

"Afraid? You aren't afraid of anything."

"Oh, yes, I am." She'd kept her hands by her sides. She could no longer do that. When she slid them around his neck, she felt his warmth seep into her. "Brand, I was afraid of what I felt for you."

He didn't speak; his eyes asked the question.

"I shouldn't love you. It was all wrong. That's what I believed. Then." Her words sounded disjointed. She felt disjointed. "Falling in love with you was the last thing I expected. The last I wanted."

"But it happened?"

Her vision had blurred while she searched her heart for what she needed to say. When she blinked and focused, Brand was waiting for her—not with words but with a clean, clear message in his eyes.

He loved her.

He understood how vulnerable, off balance, and awe-struck she felt, because the same thing had happened to him.

"Tonight?" Her lips ached to feel his mouth pressed against them, instead of words being forced past them. "You want me to go back with you tonight?"

"Yes. Please."

He was coming closer, the movement smooth and sure. She tilted her head upward and stood on tiptoe. He held her against his length, giving her something to support herself with.

"There's nothing I want more," she answered him.

"Oh, Kara. Kara, I love you."

"And I love you."

She felt his fingers press against the small of her back, and she increased her hold on his neck. Then they were so close that she could no longer make out his features.

But it didn't matter. Her body knew what he felt like. So did her heart.

SHARE THE FUN . . .
SHARE YOUR NEW-FOUND TREASURE!!

You don't want to let your new books out of your sight? That's okay. Your friends can get their own. Order below.

No. 63 **WHERE THERE'S A WILL** by Leanne Banks
Chelsea goes toe-to-toe with her new, unhappy business partner.

No. 64 **YESTERDAY'S FANTASY** by Pamela Macaluso
Melissa always had a crush on Morgan. Maybe dreams do come true!

No. 65 **TO CATCH A LORELEI** by Phyllis Houseman
Lorelei sets a trap for Daniel but gets caught in it herself.

No. 66 **BACK OF BEYOND** by Shirley Faye
Dani and Jesse are forced to face their true feelings for each other.

No. 67 **CRYSTAL CLEAR** by Cay David
Max could be the end of all Chrystal's dreams . . . or just the beginning!

No. 68 **PROMISE OF PARADISE** by Karen Lawton Barrett
Gabriel is surprised to find that Eden's beauty is not just skin deep.

No. 69 **OCEAN OF DREAMS** by Patricia Hagan
Is Jenny just another shipboard romance to Officer Kirk Moen?

No. 70 **SUNDAY KIND OF LOVE** by Lois Faye Dyer
Trace literally sweeps beautiful, ebony-haired Lily off her feet.

Meteor Publishing Corporation
Dept. 393, P. O. Box 41820, Philadelphia, PA 19101-9828

Please send the books I've indicated below. Check or money order (U.S. Dollars only)—no cash, stamps or C.O.D.s (PA residents, add 6% sales tax). I am enclosing $2.95 plus 75¢ handling fee for *each* book ordered.

Total Amount Enclosed: $_____.

___ No. 48	___ No. 53	___ No. 59	___ No. 65
___ No. 135	___ No. 54	___ No. 60	___ No. 66
___ No. 49	___ No. 55	___ No. 61	___ No. 67
___ No. 50	___ No. 56	___ No. 62	___ No. 68
___ No. 51	___ No. 57	___ No. 63	___ No. 69
___ No. 52	___ No. 58	___ No. 64	___ No. 70

Please Print:
Name _____
Address _____ Apt. No. _____
City/State _____ Zip _____

Allow four to six weeks for delivery. Quantities limited.